D0309985

04167718 - ITEM

SPECIAL MESSAGE TO READERS

THE ULVERSCROFT FOUNDATION
(registered UK charity number 264873)

was established in 1972 to provide funds for research, diagnosis and treatment of eye diseases.
Examples of major projects funded by the Ulverscroft Foundation are:-

- The Children's Eye Unit at Moorfields Eye Hospital, London
- The Ulverscroft Children's Eye Unit at Great Ormond Street Hospital for Sick Children
- Funding research into eye diseases and treatment at the Department of Ophthalmology, University of Leicester
- The Ulverscroft Vision Research Group, Institute of Child Health
- Twin operating theatres at the Western Ophthalmic Hospital, London
- The Chair of Ophthalmology at the Royal Australian College of Ophthalmologists

You can help further the work of the Foundation by making a donation or leaving a legacy.
Every contribution is gratefully received. If you would like to help support the Foundation or require further information, please contact:

THE ULVERSCROFT FOUNDATION
The Green, Bradgate Road, Anstey
Leicester LE7 7FU, England
Tel: (0116) 236 4325
website: www.foundation.ulverscroft.com

KILLING COUSINS

Suburban housewife Willie Hogan is selfish, bored, and beautiful, passing her time at the country club and having casual affairs. Her husband Howard doesn't seem to care particularly — until one night she comes home from a party to discover he has packed his things and intends to leave her for good. Panicked, Willie grabs Howard's gun and shoots him dead. With the help of her current paramour, Howard's clever cousin Quincy, the body is disposed of — but unbeknownst to either of them, their problems are only just beginning . . .

FLETCHER FLORA

KILLING COUSINS

Complete and Unabridged

LINFORD
Leicester

First published in Great Britain

First Linford Edition
published 2016

Copyright © 1950 by Fletcher Flora
All rights reserved

A catalogue record for this book is available
from the British Library.

ISBN 978–1–4448–2950–1

EAST SUSSEX COUNTY LIBRARY	
04167718	
ULV	1 9 ??? 2016
	£8.99
EAST SUSSEX CC	

1

The town of Quivera, in spite of its intrusion upon a legend, is not an exceptional town; and Ouichita Road, which is a street in Quivera, is not an exceptional street. There was a time, however, when it tried to be, and the signs of the attempt are still apparent. It is eight winding blocks of black macadam, narrow and tree-lined, in an area that achieves an atmosphere of indigenous rusticity. This atmosphere, not really so much achieved as retained, is due to a lack of artificial landscaping and a vague agreement among Ouichita property owners to preserve as much as possible the natural growth of the area. Oaks and maples and sycamores and elms and dogwood and redbud are thick on the deep lawns that slope rather steeply to the street on both sides, and the houses appear to have been dropped down among them casually. The rusticity thus preserved somehow manages, ironically, to seem more artificial than any amount of designing and planting would have made it.

There are a few very expensive houses on Ouichita Road, but most of them are not. Most of them are only moderately pretentious, and were built by people in the upper-middle-income bracket who were willing to risk a bigger mortgage than they could comfortably carry. The same people drive a somewhat bigger car than they ought to drive. Or, if they do not, drive two smaller ones, one of which is usually a Renault or a Volkswagen or an MG or something else of foreign extraction. They operate shops, work in banks, sell insurance and real estate, practice professions. They usually belong to the country club, and occasionally become delinquent in the payment of their dues. They think of themselves as rather more sophisticated than the average run of Quiverans, and perhaps they are. On Ouichita Road there is a high incidence of marginal promiscuity, a lower incidence of adultery.

Several Ouichita Road residents have achieved fame. One, a lawyer by the name of Chalmers, is remembered as the only

Republican candidate for governor to be defeated in a period of thirty years. Another, the daughter of a certified public accountant, went to Hollywood and appeared briefly in two Westerns, in one of which she was photographed in the proximity of John Wayne. Still another, the nephew of the gubernatorial candidate and eventually the husband of the actress, was an All-American tackle at the state university, and played two seasons with the Pittsburgh Steelers before coming home to sell insurance for his mother's cousin.

But the most famous by far of all Ouichita Road residents, or all Quiverans together, was Mrs. Willie Hogan.

Willie committed murder.

2

On the morning of a certain day, which was a day that was different from any other day there ever was, Willie sat Indian-fashion on the floor of her bedroom at 524 Ouichita Road and painted her fingernails. She planned, after finishing the fingernails, to paint her toenails. The nails had been a delicate coral in color when she started, but the coral had been removed, and she was now in the process of applying a coat of scarlet. The reason she was so engaged — applying the bright lacquer in the first place, and such a bold color in the second — was that she had a problem that needed thinking about, and a feeling of depression that needed the alleviative of something especially cheerful.

Willie always painted her nails when she felt compelled to think very long or very hard about a problem. This was a practice she had picked up from her father, who had been a brakeman on a railroad. Whenever her father had felt particularly oppressed and defeated by accumulated bills, or his wife, or his own deficiencies, or anything whatever, he had painted a high board fence along the alley behind their house. Painting, he said, soothed his mind and reduced his troubles to proper perspective. Sometimes he painted the fence one color, sometimes another. It depended on the quality of the trouble he was currently having.

Willie had no fence to paint, and wouldn't have painted it in any case, but she had discovered that she could achieve the same therapy by painting her nails. Painting nails was truly a meticulous task, and it required considerable artistry to do it properly. Once she became committed, the quality of her work assumed such enormous importance in her mind that other matters were diminished in comparison. Thus diminished, they seemed more manageable.

Willie's problem was Howard. Howard was Willie's husband. A lot of people who lived on Ouichita Road could not understand why she had ever married him, or why, having married him, she perversely insisted upon keeping him. These were all people, however, who had always lived on Ouichita Road, or on streets comparable in quality. Willie hadn't. She had lived, before marrying Howard, in another town in a residential area where, if the mortgages were smaller, the accommodations were plainly inferior. One of seven in a five-room house on a narrow lot that was allergic to grass, the only bright thing she could remember in that time was the alley fence that her father kept painting different colors. She couldn't remember that he had ever painted the house.

Anyhow, all things considered, she had seen Howard, who was the only son of a prosperous beer distributor, as a glamorous figure against an esoteric background. He lived in a house that was two-and-a-half stories high and had wall-to-wall carpeting all over, except in the kitchen and bathrooms; and when he had taken her there for dinner one evening, served by a maid, she had lost entirely what little capacity for critical evaluation she had had previously, if she had had any at all. It was quite impossible then, at the age of nineteen, for her to see that he, at the age of twenty-three, was really an amiable lubber who already showed signs of looking like King Farouk. Shortly afterward she seduced him so subtly that he was left with the conviction that it had been the other way around. After the event, in his bed alone in the two-and-a-half-story house, he kept seeing in the darkness her great grave gray eyes in her small gamin's face, and he abandoned himself so completely to a kind of spiritual orgasm of guilt and high resolves of devotion that he wound up within a month at the altar.

After marriage, Howard's tenuous glamour was soon dissipated. Willie, who was really rather shrewd and was sometimes even honest with herself, saw him clearly and good-naturedly for what he was. And what he was, to be fair about it, was acceptable enough; for he was not only reasonably prosperous by virtue of being the son of his father, but he also had, somewhat to Willie's surprise, a fortunate knack of making quite a bit of money in odd ventures without apparent benefit of skills, training, or appreciable brains. Life at 524 Ouichita Road may have been deficient with respect to the excitements and ingenuities of love, for Howard, although frequently amorous, was never ingenious and seldom effective, but it was lived at a level of comfort that was to Willie absolute luxury.

Howard's deficiency as a lover, both in looks and action, was not, in any event, a great hardship for Willie. She found, after a while, compensation elsewhere. She was a willowy little charmer with a deceptive air of innocence, and she learned to exploit her assets with skill that seemed to be based on an instinctive knowledge of what was exactly right for her in the important matters of dress and make-up and hairstyle and all the other elements of composition. In effect, although it was never so precisely analyzed, she managed to look and walk and talk in ways that subtly compromised her air of innocence without destroying it. As a result, men habitually felt for her, even after they had become experienced, a disturbing ambivalence. They wanted at once to treat her like a charming child and to go as quickly as possible to bed with her, and now they did one and now the other, according to Willie's humor at the time. Afterward, whichever way it went, they somehow always felt a strange compulsion to protect Willie's honor and reputation at any cost, if not to preserve her generosity for another occasion. And so it happened that her name was never confidentially exchanged between male members in the locker room of the Quivera Country Club, even though they may have known her intimately.

Unfortunately, Howard himself was under no illusions. In the beginning he was, and continued to be for quite a long time after the beginning; but then he had come home unexpectedly one afternoon — and it was, in Willie's opinion, a very deceitful thing to do, for it happened to be the same afternoon that she had come home earlier with Evan Spooner. She had been out to the club for a luncheon, and afterward she had gone into the bar for a

Martini or two, and as luck would have it Evan was there, having just finished nine holes of golf. It turned out he didn't have his car, and no ride back to town, so naturally he asked for a lift, which she was almost compelled to give him, especially since he paid for the Martinis. There had been three Martinis, as a matter of fact, instead of one or two, and maybe that was why she had taken Evan to her home instead of his, or somewhere else. But she seemed to remember, anyhow, that he had said rather casually that he'd just get out there and walk the rest of the way, which wasn't far, so as not to put her to a lot of trouble.

However it had happened exactly, she had brought him home with her, and it had been only common courtesy, after all, to ask him in for another Martini. The Martinis had certainly contributed to what had happened afterward, for Evan wasn't particularly somebody she wanted anything to happen to her with; but anyhow, one thing leading to another, a great deal more happened than she had expected or intended. In another ten or fifteen minutes at the most, Evan would have been gone, for she was beginning to think about sending him on his way; and it was simply the worst kind of luck that Howard, the sneak, had come home unexpectedly. But it was really not the worst kind of luck, when considered calmly, for it would have been a great deal worse if he had come five minutes earlier. Nevertheless, it was bad enough, neither she nor Evan being exactly in a state to receive any company whatever, let alone Howard; and the only lucky part about it was that you couldn't actually tell whether something had already happened or was just about to.

Willie had been angry with Howard for sneaking home that way when he wasn't expected, but at the same time she had to hand it to him for the way he behaved. He was really rather fierce in a lubberly way, and he'd actually kicked Evan right out of the house, three times on the way to the door and once going through; and afterward he had come back and slapped her so hard in the face that she fell over a chair, and had called her, in addition, a couple of names. He was positively admirable, to her surprise, and she had not much minded the slap and the names, even admitting that they were no more than he should have been allowed under the circumstances. The slap and the names were her good fortune, as it developed, inasmuch as Howard felt so guilty about them afterward that he was inclined as a consequence to feel more lenient with respect to her own guilt. She had to tell only a few lies to convince him, or nearly so, that nothing much had actually happened, and that she had been wearing more, after all, than she frequently wore publicly at the club pool.

Thereafter, however, he was never quite able to accept the postulation that her indiscretions were no more serious than the acceptable kind that were commonly committed in their set at back-yard barbecues and dances at the country club. He became, in fact, a plain nuisance. He kept watching her all the time like a private detective or something; and if she let a man hold her too tightly while dancing, or kiss her in the perfectly casual

way somebody was always kissing somebody else, or take her out across the
terrace and onto the golf course in
the dark for a breath of fresh air, why,
then he would sulk and glower the entire
rest of the evening and go into the most
ridiculous rage when they got home. This
made things tedious but not intolerable,
for she was able to seduce him each time
with only a little more difficulty than
the first time — the time before they
were married — and then things would
be all right again until the next time. This
kept happening intermittently for quite
a while, more than a year, and it was
something you learned to live with; but
then there was a change in Howard, and
you might have thought that the change
was for the better, but it was for the
worse.

The change was, Howard suddenly
didn't seem to care much any longer what
Willie did. She could fool around and
enjoy herself as much as she pleased at
the club and other places, and he never
got angry or said a word or gave a sign
that he even noticed. At first the change

was very pleasant, but then it was disturbing. When he started sleeping by himself in the bedroom on the other side of the connecting bathroom, she asked him what the matter was, but he only said nothing was the matter — that he'd got so he didn't sleep very well double; and it wasn't, anyhow, very far through the bathroom from one bedroom to the other. After the change, he had a kind of dignity about him that was rather appealing, old Howard did; and every once in a while, in the new order of things, Willie made the trip through the bathroom herself.

Another year passed after the change, more or less, and everything was pleasant enough at 524 Ouichita Road, although not very exciting, and it looked like matters had worked out and settled down into a satisfactory arrangement all around. But then last night at the club had been that little party that hadn't really been a party at all, but only something that got started and grew and happened; and what had happened, incidentally, to Willie and to Howard was something Willie didn't want to think about, but had to.

It involved another man, of course; and the man, of all people, was no one but Quincy Hogan, who was no one but Howard's own cousin.

3

It was odd about Quincy.

He was very difficult to understand, Quincy was — why he was what he was instead of something else he could have been. But the oddest thing about him, so far as Willie was concerned, was how he managed to make her feel the way he did when, if you stopped to consider it, he shouldn't have made her feel that way at all.

He simply wasn't the type of man who normally appealed to her, or had begun to appeal to her after she had established a satisfactory financial and social position by marrying Howard, who wasn't the type either. The men who normally appealed to her were the ones who played golf and maybe tennis, and swam afterward in the club pool in those brief little trunks that made the most interesting break in their sun-browned bodies. And it didn't make any difference that they really weren't much good at any of those things, just so long as they carried themselves with the proper air of superiority, as when walking across the terrace with the cleats, or whatever you called the things on the soles of their golf shoes, making arrogant little clicking sounds on the concrete, or when talking loudly about birdies and par and things like that over highballs and gins-and-tonics and Moscow Mules in the bar.

Quincy didn't play golf or tennis or swim in the pool, and the only thing he had in common with most of the men who did was a remarkable capacity for the refreshments of the bar, particularly bourbon on the rocks. And in this respect, Willie had to admit, he was even superior to the others, for he commonly spent hours developing it in that air-conditioned haven while they were otherwise occupied in the hot sun outside.

What Quincy was, was a brain. As a child, Willie had been told, he worked difficult mathematics problems in his head and could remember a whole page of reading after one time over. What he also was, was poor. He'd gone off to the state university on a scholarship or something, and there he'd amazed the professors and graduated *cum laude*, whatever that meant. And then he'd come immediately home to Quivera and got a job as teller in the City National Bank; and that's where he still was and what he still was — still a brain and still poor, and not caring a single damn, apparently, about being anywhere or anything else.

Weekends, he was usually at the club, dividing his time among the bar, where he drank and drank and got quietly drunk; and the slot-machine room, where he played for quarters and always won; and the terrace outside, where he lay in a sling chair and slept or read thick books about all sorts of peculiar things like science and history and philosophy and such. He wasn't even good-looking by acceptable standards. He was short and slim, moving with a kind of indolent grace, but he had a nose twisted to one side and a mouth twisted to the other, and his skin was dark and very slightly pocked in the face by something he had had as a child.

He was certainly a brain, all right, though brains were not highly regarded by Willie unless they were applied to the accumulation of material advantages. Old Howard, for instance, didn't have much of a brain, but he had this knack for making two dollars out of one; and that, in Willie's opinion, was a hell of a lot more important. Anyhow, all things considered, it was simply incredible that Quincy made her feel the way he did, and the way he made her feel was kind of breathless and prickly and ready. She'd got acquainted with him early, of course, since he was Howard's cousin, the son of the brother of Howard's father. It was perfectly clear that he held Howard in contempt — perfectly clear to everyone but Howard; and this had made Willie hostile in the beginning, more because it was an incidental reflection on her than for Howard's sake. She kept telling herself that Quincy was really rather ridiculous — all brains and no glands — and for a long time this was something she almost believed, in spite of the ready feeling. But then had come a particular night at the club, which was shortly after the unfortunate episode with Evan Spooner; and after that it wasn't possible to almost believe it any longer.

It was a Friday night, and there were some people outside swimming in the pool and sitting around on the terrace, and some more people dancing to the jukebox and sitting around at tables in the bar, and Howard was at one of the tables in a game of gin rummy. It happened that Willie had gone to the powder room, which was next to the slot-machine room, and she could hear a machine playing in there. Looking in to see who was playing it, she saw that it was Quincy. He was standing there with a bourbon in one hand and a cigarette hanging loosely from his lips, and he'd put in a quarter and pull the handle and reach into his jacket pocket for another quarter while the drum was still spinning, and as soon as the drum had stopped he'd put in the other quarter and pull the handle again. He didn't win anything while Willie was watching, and pretty soon she went in and stood beside him and slightly behind him, so close that they touched when he turned half around to see who she was.

'Hello, Quincy,' she said.

'Hello, Cousin,' he said, turning away again and putting another quarter into the machine.

'Any luck?'

'Only bad.'

'Maybe I could change it.'

'You think so? Pull the handle.'

She pulled the handle, and it was one of those breaks of pure luck that sometimes come. The drum spun and quit spinning, and there, sure enough, were three of a kind lined up as neatly as you could wish. The machine gave a kind of metallic belch and spilled a jackpot of quarters into the coin receptacle below.

'Well, I'll be damned,' Quincy said. 'No wonder old Howard just keeps getting richer and richer.'

'It was nothing but luck,' Willie said.

'I know.' He looked at her over his shoulder, his nose twisting one way and his mouth the other, and he gave an added twist to the twist of his mouth that made a kind of smile of it. 'What's better than luck?' He put another quarter into the machine and pulled the handle to take the jackpot off. Then he began to take the quarters out of the receptacle and drop them into his jacket pocket.

'Are you quitting?' she said.

'Why not? No use playing a machine that just dumped the jackpot.'

'Oh, yes. That's true, isn't it? Well, if you are going to quit, I may as well leave. I think I'll go upstairs and outside for a while.'

'Wait a minute. The pot's yours. I'll get it changed into paper at the bar for you.'

'Don't be absurd. I simply won't hear of it. It was your quarter I played with.'

'We'll split, then. Down the middle. Nine dollars apiece.'

'Not at all. You must keep it all for yourself.'

'I want you to have half. If you won't have it, I'll throw it all into the swimming pool.'

She thought that he was surely just the one who would do it, and she kept having all the while that peculiar prickly feeling that she shouldn't have had. He was short for a man, a kind of runt, and they were practically the same height when she was wearing high heels, as she now was. He stared levelly into her eyes, nowhere else, but she had suddenly a new feeling, which was part of the larger prickliness, that the high heels were *all* she was wearing.

'All right,' she said. 'If you want me to have half, I'll have it.'

She turned and walked out and upstairs into a hall and from there onto a terrace, which was ground level on the front, just as the terrace downstairs was ground level on the back, the club being built on a slope that made things turn out that way. She had thought that he would follow her, which was what she wanted, but he wasn't behind her and didn't come, and after a minute or two of waiting she began to feel rejected and humiliated and slightly angry.

But then he was there beside her, having come, after all. 'What are you doing up here?' she said.

'Following you. What are you doing?'

'Waiting for you.'

'So here we are, Cousin.'

'I was beginning to think you weren't coming.'

'Well, hell, you didn't expect me to walk around with five pounds of quarters in my pocket, did you?'

'Where shall we go?'

'Let's go down and sit in old Howard's new Buick.'

'What shall we do?'

'If it suits you, we can make love.'

So that's where they went and what they did; and afterward, back in the club, he gave her nine dollars, half of the pot. She didn't think anything about it at the time; but later, remembering it, it seemed almost like she was being paid, and she wondered if he'd done it that way deliberately, the ugly little bastard.

Anyhow, it was certainly strange about Quincy. After that night, which was understandable as an experience that just sort of happened, you'd have thought she'd have forgotten about him in favor of the type of man that normally appealed to her, but that wasn't what developed; and what developed was something Willie

24

couldn't seem to help. After that night, as a matter of fact, it was exclusively Quincy, except Howard now and then, and one time one other; and there had even been a couple of weekends in KC.

Everything had gone along without any serious difficulties or problems, and Willie didn't think there was actually much risk to it, for no one would reasonably suspect her of having an affair with Quincy, of all people. But then last night, quite the contrary, everything had gone suddenly all to pieces. And was still in pieces; and she couldn't see any way, for the life of her, to put the pieces together again.

This was Saturday morning; and last night had been Friday, just like the first night, with Quincy, and at the club there had been another one of those little parties that just get started and grow. Willie had been there with Howard, and Quincy had been there alone, and a lot of others had been there too, mostly married couples. There was a lot of dancing to the jukebox, with people passing partners around, as well as quite a lot of drinking as the night went on. Quite a lot of drinking was unavoidable, really, because someone always bought a round of drinks, which made everyone else obligated to buy a round of drinks before the party was over. And so many rounds of drinks just naturally added up to quite a lot of drinking that was unavoidable as a matter of obligation.

Willie danced and danced, and Howard was agreeable and didn't seem to mind. Quincy stood with his elbows on the bar and drank bourbon and didn't dance with anyone, not even Willie; for he considered dancing, like golf and tennis, an unreasonable exertion.

After midnight, about half past, Quincy turned away from the bar and faced the room, his elbows still bracing him behind, and after a few minutes walked out and up the stairs without saying a word to anyone. Howard at the moment was talking and laughing with two men in a corner, maybe telling dirty stories. Willie said 'Excuse me' to the man she happened to be dancing with and went into the powder room, next to the slot-machine room, in case someone happened to be watching. After a minute or so, she slipped out and upstairs after Quincy and found him standing on the terrace.

They walked down along a row of parked cars and off at an angle across the golf course in the dark. They must have walked back that way a hundred yards or more to a large sycamore tree, and so much time was spent there pleasantly under the tree after arriving that it was past one when they got back to the bar in the club, and Howard was gone.

Well, Quincy had taken her home in his second-hand Plymouth, and she had been furious with Howard for being so unreasonable and mean. She had gone upstairs and directly into his room with the intention of telling him precisely what she thought of him for deserting her — and there he was with the lights burning and a large leather bag open on the bed. He was plainly putting clothes into the bag with the purpose of going away somewhere.

'Hello,' he said pleasantly. 'Did you and Quincy have a good lay?'

This was disconcerting, to say the least. Willie had carefully planned the very first thing she was going to say, for it was important to get off to a good start in matters of this kind. But now she was compelled to change her position in the last instant, and the new position was defensive, instead of offensive, which was bad.

'What in the world are you talking about?' she said.

'You know what I'm talking about,' he said, 'and don't bother to tell me any lies, because it won't do you any good. I know damn well what's been going on between you and Quincy.'

'Do you actually? In that case, perhaps you wouldn't mind telling me what it is, for if anything at all has been going on between us, I don't know it.'

'Never mind. You're a natural-born liar, and would keep on denying it even if I had photographs. The truth is, I don't care, and I don't want to talk about it.'

In the meantime, while talking, he walked over to a chest and took some socks and underwear out of an open drawer and returned with them to the leather bag and put them in. He didn't look at her anymore, after the first time, and he had about him that lubberly kind of dignity that she had noticed before on certain occasions. The most disturbing thing about him was that he clearly wasn't in the least angry, and there was even a special kind of lightheartedness in his attitude, as if he had made up his mind about something and was relieved as a consequence.

'What are you doing?' she said.

'As you can see, I'm packing.'

'Where are you going?'

'I'm going away.'

''Away' is no answer. Where, exactly, away?'

'That's none of your business. Wherever it is, though, I'm never coming back, and you can be certain of that.'

'Don't be absurd.'

'You may think I'm absurd if you choose. You'll see.'

'Well, if you are determined to accuse me falsely of having an affair with your own cousin, who is an ugly little devil besides, there's nothing I care to say to you. And if you want to run away and leave me, there's nothing I can do to stop you. You'll be sorry after a while for treating me so unfairly. When you come back, I hope you'll be prepared to be sensible.'

'I said I'm not coming back, and I'm not.'

'Excuse me, please. I'm tired, and I believe I'll go to bed.'

She went through the bathroom into her own bedroom, where she took off all her clothes and put on a pale blue nightgown that practically wasn't there. Then, after brushing her teeth and her hair and repairing her face, she went back through the bathroom into the other bedroom and stood between Howard and a light. He glanced at her once and quickly away.

'You needn't try that either,' he said.

'Try what, may I ask?' she said.

'Coming in here trying to seduce me. It won't work this time.'

'You're talking very strangely, I must say. Are you sure you're not drunk?

Surely a wife has the right to wear her nightgown in the presence of her husband without being accused of all sorts of things.'

'Oh, hell! What's the use? I'm going away, that's all, and I'm not coming back. Nothing more is to be said or done.'

She was convinced then that he was telling the simple truth, that he was going and wouldn't return, and she was instantly aware of the immensity of her possible loss. She could perhaps make arrangements for herself that would equal the house at 524 Ouichita Road and the country club and two cars and all the exciting associations with men who played golf and tennis and ordered rounds of drinks like nothing at all. But on the other hand, possibly she couldn't. And what, if she couldn't, would ever become of her? She had a clear vision of a narrow, bleak house in a bare yard before a bright board fence, and she felt a terrible loneliness and a cold, cold fear.

'You can't go,' she said.

'I can,' he said, 'and I will.'

'I won't let you.'

'You can't stop me.'

'We'll see if I can't.'

Her head was spinning round and round, which caused the room to spin as well, or seem to, and the truth was that she was still pretty tight from all the rounds of drinks at the club. The one idea that got fixed in her mind clearly was that Howard kept a little revolver in the drawer of the night table beside his bed, and that she could surely use this revolver in some way, if she had it, to persuade Howard not to go away.

She went over to the table and opened the drawer; and there, sure enough, was the revolver. She picked it up and held it in her hand. Howard was watching her.

'What are you doing with that?' he said.

'Maybe I'll kill myself.'

'Go ahead. It's loaded.'

'You wish I would, don't you?'

'Not particularly. It doesn't matter one way or another.'

'Maybe I'll kill you instead.'

'I'm not worried about it.'

'No? You think I won't do it?'

'No.'

'What makes you so sure?'

'You haven't got the nerve. You haven't got the nerve to kill yourself or me or anyone at all.'

'Be careful. You may be wrong.'

'Go ahead, then. Kill me.'

'You'd like to see me in trouble, wouldn't you?'

'If you get into trouble by killing me, I won't be around to see it.'

'You don't care what happens to me, do you?'

'Yes, I do, as a matter of fact. I wish you all the bad luck in the world. I hope you go right back to the poor trash I took you away from, and I don't doubt you will.'

If he had been trying deliberately to say exactly the wrong thing, he couldn't have done better. He was standing suddenly against a garish fence, bright blue at this time, and she shot him. He fell back against the fence and sat down with an expression of complete astonishment on his face. He sat there for a second or two, and then lay down sidewise beside the fence and did not move thereafter.

It was such a little revolver, hardly more than a toy; and Willie was, moreover, such a bad shot, that it was a kind of miracle that she should have hit him at all, let alone in a vital place. It was purely by chance, in fact, that she did. It must have been his heart, the vital place, for there was a little hole in his shirt just over the place where his heart probably was.

She walked over and looked down at him, but did not touch him, and she was certain that he was dead. It was incredible that Howard should simply be dead so suddenly; something she could not immediately adjust to.

Her head kept on spinning, and she thought that she probably ought to do something, but she couldn't think of anything specific that would do the least bit of good. It would be much better to consider the problem when she could think clearly, and in the meanwhile it would be necessary to arrive at a condition where clear thinking was possible.

She went back through the bathroom into her own bedroom, still carrying the little gun, which she placed on the table beside her bed, and lay down to rest a few minutes. She must have gone almost immediately to sleep, for the next she knew, it was morning, this morning, the morning of Saturday, and Howard was dead in his bedroom beside a blue fence.

Howard dead was Willie's problem, and the crux of the problem was what to do with him.

4

Having finished her fingers, she began on her toes. Bending forward from the hips, she applied herself earnestly to the meticulous work; and as she worked she considered carefully her problem and its possible solutions.

Her mind was quite clear now, after several hours of sleep, and she did not feel, strangely enough, the least bit of urgency. When she had first wakened and remembered what had happened, she had been very frightened and had felt a necessity to do something immediately, no matter what. But then it had occurred to her that it all might be nothing more than a bad dream, which she sometimes had. And so she had gone into Howard's bedroom to make sure, one way or the other; and it had turned out not to be a dream at all, for there Howard was on the floor.

Instead of increasing her fright and

making her do something precipitate that might have turned out badly, the sight of him had worked just the opposite effect and had made her suddenly calm and thoughtful. She had thought first of Mrs. Tweedy, the woman who came in daily to clean and cook; but by a stroke of good luck Mrs. Tweedy had asked for the day off and would not be in, so nothing needed to be done about calling her and telling her not to come, or anything like that. This seemed to remove all the urgency from the matter, and Willie had returned to her own bedroom, where she now was, and had begun to do her nails, which she was still doing.

The disposal of Howard in a way that would not be prejudicial to her own interests would really be quite a difficult task, and she was prepared to admit that she probably couldn't accomplish it alone. What she needed was help, and the one she kept thinking about as a helper was Quincy.

Quincy was a brain — that was generally acknowledged — and no doubt, if consulted, he would be simply teeming with ideas about what to do. The question was, could he be trusted in a matter this delicate? He was no better than he ought to be, certainly, but Willie was not convinced that he had the necessary intestinal fortitude.

Nevertheless, there was no thinkable alternative. She must trust Quincy, or no one. By the time she had finished her toes she had resolved to call him and ask him to come over at once. Because it was Saturday, he would not be working at the bank, and it was almost certain, early as it was, that he was still in bed in the depressing little apartment he kept and in which she had been once or twice against her better judgment.

Getting up, she went into the bathroom and put the little bottle of scarlet lacquer away neatly in the cabinet where she kept it. Then she went back through her bedroom and out into the hall to the telephone, an extension. She was just reaching for it, remembering the digits in Quincy's number, when it began to ring. She picked it up and answered, and she could tell at once from the voice, which was like no other voice in the entire world, that it was Howard's mother.

'Is that you, Willie?' Howard's mother said.

'Yes, it is,' Willie said. 'It's me.'

'How are you this morning, my dear?'

Mother Hogan always called Willie her dear, but it was more in patronage than in affection; a motherly tolerance of a son's inexplicable mistake. Willie hated Mother Hogan's insides, and she thought now that it was really a shame it wasn't Mother Hogan who had to be disposed of, instead of Howard.

'I'm all right,' she said. 'I'm fine.'

'Is Howard there?'

'He's here, but I don't think he can come to the phone.'

'Can't come? Whyever not?'

'Well, he's still sleeping.'

'No matter, my dear. Just wake him up.'

'I don't believe I can do that.'

'My dear, you're being particularly difficult, if you don't mind my saying so. Of course you can wake him up. What's to stop you?'

'As a matter of fact, he's sick.'

'Sick? What's the matter with him?'

'Well, he had too much to drink last night, and he's got a bad headache and this terribly upset stomach.'

'Howard had too much to drink? Nonsense, my dear. Howard *never* has too much to drink.'

'Sometimes he does, and last night he did.'

'Have you called Dr. Wheeler?'

'It isn't necessary to call a doctor for a hangover.'

'Hangover indeed! I'm positive Howard has no such thing. Really, Willie, you would probably let him lie right there and die of something serious and insist all the time that he'd only had too much to drink.'

'He doesn't have anything serious, damn it. He only has a hangover.'

'You needn't swear at me, Willie.'

'Did I swear? I'm sorry.'

'I'm coming right over to see how Howard is. I'll be there immediately.'

'No, no. That's not possible.'

'What?'

'You can't come.'

'Are you being deliberately offensive, Willie?'

'Oh, well, I see that I may as well tell you the truth.'

'I should hope so.'

'The truth is, Howard's not here.'

'Where is he?'

'I don't know. We had a quarrel last night after getting home from the club, and he left.'

'That doesn't sound like Howard at all. You must have driven him to it, Willie.'

'Well, anyhow, he left, and he's not here.'

'It's strange that he didn't come home.'

'Perhaps he'll come there later.'

'That's true. He didn't want to disturb me last night, of course. Probably he went to a hotel, or to a friend's.'

'You needn't worry about him, in any case. He's perfectly capable of taking care of himself.'

'Willie, you've never understood Howard in the least, and you ought to be ashamed of yourself for upsetting him so.'

'Do you think so? When it comes to

that, I'm somewhat upset myself, so if you don't mind, I don't believe I care to continue this conversation any longer.'

She hung up and kept on standing there by the telephone. It was obvious now that she must quit thinking and start doing something at once, for there was no telling who might come and cause all sorts of inconvenience, if not genuine trouble.

Again she thought about the digits of Quincy's number, then picked up the phone and dialed them. She could hear the bell ringing at the other end of the line. After three rings, Quincy came on.

'Quincy,' Willie said, 'you can't imagine how happy I am to find you in.'

'Are you? Since last night I've been thinking you might not be feeling so amiable toward me.'

'Whatever gave you such a fantastic idea? Why shouldn't I be feeling amiable toward you?'

'Well, with old Howard cutting out the way he did, I had a notion you might be in for a bad time when you got home.'

'Howard was angry, all right, I'll not

deny that. He accused me of all sorts of things.'

'What sorts of things?'

'You know. Being unfaithful and all that.'

'I see. You mean he accused you of being what you were.'

'Are you trying to be unpleasantly funny about it, Quincy? If you are, I wish you wouldn't.'

'Sorry, Cousin. Is old Howard actually on to us?'

'It's my opinion he was just guessing and making assumptions and such.'

'That's a relief. I thought maybe you were calling to warn me to get out of town.'

'Nothing of the sort. What I've called you for is to ask you to come over here as quickly as possible.'

'Over to your house?'

'Certainly.'

'Are you crazy?'

'Of course I'm not crazy. I'm thinking very clearly, as a matter of fact, and under the circumstances that's quite exceptional.'

'Well, I'm not crazy either, Cousin, and I'm thinking just as clearly as you are. And what I'm clearly thinking is that your house is not at present one of the places I ought to come to.'

'You must, Quincy. It's essential.'

'Look, Cousin, I'm just a little guy. I'm damned if I'm coming over there and get slammed around by a big slob like Howard.'

'You needn't worry about that. Howard isn't here.'

'He might come back.'

'No, he won't. I promise you.'

'How do you know he won't?'

'I just know, that's all.'

'I don't think I'll take a chance on it.'

'Damn it, Quincy, please don't be so contrary. Something has happened that I can't tell you about on the telephone, and you must come right over.'

'You're sure Howard won't come back?'

'I'm sure. I promise he won't, and he won't.'

'In that case, I'll come.'

He hung up abruptly, and Willie stood

for a few seconds listening to the hum of the dead wire. Then she went back into her bedroom and sat down on the edge of the bed and began waiting for Quincy.

5

A half-hour had passed before he came. The little ivory clock on Willie's dressing table said exactly nine-thirty when the doorbell downstairs began to ring, and she continued to sit on the edge of the bed in the belief that Quincy would surely show enough initiative to open the door and come in, but he didn't.

After an interval of silence, the bell began to ring again, and Willie got up and went out into the hall and started downstairs. She was almost all the way down when she became aware that she was still wearing the thin blue nightgown that was practically nothing. She should have dressed, she thought, for she didn't want to get Quincy unnecessarily agitated or diverted from the business at hand. But it was too late now. If she took the time to go back and put on clothes, or even a robe, it was entirely possible that Quincy, who was an impatient little devil, might tire of waiting and go away. On bare feet, her bright nails shining, she crossed the lower hall to the front door and let Quincy in.

'Well,' he said, staring at her, 'it's apparent that Howard's not here, as you said.'

'To be honest,' she said, 'I only told you half the truth. It's not true that he's not here, but it's true that you needn't worry about it.'

'On the contrary, I'm worried already. Goodbye, please.'

'Oh, let me explain, Quincy. Please don't be such a coward.'

'I'm not a coward. I'm a realist. I'm little and Howard's big, and it's only sensible to stay out of his way until I know how he intends to behave.'

'Damn it, Quincy, if you will only be quiet for just a minute! There's no need to worry about Howard because he's dead.'

For an instant Quincy merely looked slightly stupid, which was a way Quincy rarely looked. But then his eyes began to shine, and Willie could tell that he was intensely interested, although somewhat leery. 'That's a refreshing way to look at it,' he said.

'Oh, you know what I mean. I mean he can't beat you up or make trouble for you or do anything like that.'

'If he's dead, he certainly can't beat me up, but there's a chance he could make a hell of a lot more trouble for me than he ever could alive. You wouldn't pull my leg, would you, Cousin?'

'Certainly not. It's no joking matter. I tell you, Howard's up in his room dead on the floor, and that's what I wanted to see you about. I want you to advise me what to do with him.'

'I'm not sure I should. In fact, I'm sure I ought to turn around and get the hell out of here.'

'You can desert me if you choose, but I didn't think you'd ever do it when I was in trouble and needed you.'

His eyes were shining brighter and brighter, and it was obvious that he was excited. He was breathing faster than normal, and he began to pick at his lower lip with the thumb and index finger of his right hand.

'I'll admit I find the situation challenging,' he said. 'Do you mind if I go up and have a look at old Howard?'

'Not at all,' she said. 'I'll show you the way.'

She went ahead of him up the stairs in her thin gown, and this was something that would certainly have been quite a diversion at another time, but now he was affected only to the degree of making a vague sort of mental note that it was something that might be attended to later.

They went into Willie's room and through the bathroom into Howard's room, and Quincy walked over and bent over Howard and examined him intently for several seconds. 'He's dead, all right,' he said. 'Old Howard's dead enough.'

'Of course he's dead. He's been dead for hours.'

'That's apparent from his condition. Rigor mortis, I mean. Old Howard's stiff as a board.' Quincy straightened up and nudged the body gently with a toe. 'Rigor mortis is quite an interesting phenomenon, you know. Doctors frequently estimate the time of death from it. It's caused by coagulation of proteins in the muscles, and generally lasts about twenty-four hours. When did old Howard die, exactly?'

'It was about two o'clock, I think. I don't remember very clearly when I got home, or how long afterward it was when he died.'

'Well, it will certainly be after midnight, anyhow, before old Howard begins to limber up. He will require that long to reach a sufficiently advanced state of bacterial decomposition and essential acidity.'

'Damn it, Quincy, is it necessary to be quite so clinical?'

'It does no harm to think precisely, especially if you are trying to avoid being hanged. In my judgment, Howard was shot through the heart by a small-caliber gun.'

'There's no need to exercise your judgment about it at all. He was shot with the little revolver he kept in the drawer of the table beside his bed, and I shot him.'

'I assumed as much. Very neatly done,

too, Cousin. I didn't dream that you were such a sharpshooter.'

'It was an accident, really. I couldn't do it again in a million years.'

'No matter. The big thing about having killed someone is that it's never *necessary* to do it again. If you don't mind my asking, what compelled you to shoot old Howard? He was a rather inoffensive fellow, to be fair about it, and I should have thought that under the circumstances, if someone was going to shoot someone, it would have happened just the other way around.'

'Well, he was packing when I got home, as you can see by the bag on the bed and the two on the floor that he'd already packed before. He simply wouldn't listen to reason and was determined to leave me, and so I got the gun and shot him to prevent it.'

'There's a certain convincing illogic in that, Cousin. I believe you.'

'Why shouldn't you believe me? It's the simple truth. Anyhow, I can't see what's to be gained by talking and talking about it. Howard's dead, and I killed him. The question is, what's to be done about it?'

'You have got yourself into a tough spot, Cousin.'

'Please don't lecture me as if I were a child or something, Quincy. I know very well that I'm in a difficult position, and that's why I asked you to come over and advise me. You're very clever, as everyone knows, and I was certain that you could think of something helpful.'

'Thanks very much. Incidentally, of course, I can make myself an accessory after the fact of murder.'

'I must say, Quincy, that you're being a big disappointment to me. If you're going to start weaseling and trying to think of every possible reason for not helping me, you may as well go away at once and leave me to do the best I can without you.'

Quincy turned and walked over to the bed and sat down. He did not seem to be offended about Howard. All the while Willie stood and stared at Quincy, and she knew from his shining eyes, in spite of what he might say, that he was still interested and excited and would surely help her for the satisfaction of being clever, if for no other reason. He kept picking at his lower lip, and was apparently thinking intently.

'Let's consider the possibilities,' he said. 'To begin with, we must either explain Howard or remove him. Explaining him at this stage of the game would be, I'm afraid, extremely difficult, if not impossible. Consider the position of self-defense, for instance. You might have assumed such a position if you'd acted in time. Old Howard was drunk. He was furious. He was temporarily out of a mind that was not too reliable at best. He threatened to kill you and came at you with the clear intent. In fear of your life, you snatched the little gun out of the drawer and shot him. This would have required some preparation and some pretty good acting, but it would have required most of all that you call the cops at once. After all, old Howard is hardly smoking from death and violence lately done. As a matter of fact, he's cold as a stone and stiff as a board.

'I'm afraid it would prejudice your case when it became known that you calmly lay down and had a good night's sleep after doing old Howard in. I'm bound to tell you, Cousin, that you've bungled the business badly in the matter of establishing the basis of an acceptable explanation.'

'You needn't be smug and critical, just the same. After what happened, besides all the drinks at the club, you could hardly expect me to think clearly.'

'I was merely making an observation, Cousin, and it must be repeated in other connections. Let's consider the case for an accident. Old Howard was just the kind of lubberly fathead who would be likely to have an accident if he started fooling around with a gun or anything the least dangerous. You could have made a beautiful case for an accident if you had thought clearly and acted promptly. I admit that there would have been certain technical difficulties, such as the absence of powder burn and the position of the wound, but they could have been avoided or surmounted, especially if you had consulted me in time. Almost any imbecility would have been believed of Howard. Any number of people would have testified that he was just the one to kill himself accidentally in a way that would have been impossible to anyone else. There's no use thinking about it now, however; it's much too late.'

'Couldn't I say I didn't hear the shot and didn't discover Howard until today? After all, he was home before me and slept in a different room, and it would have been entirely possible. I frequently didn't see him from one night to the next.'

'No, no.' Quincy shook his head and pinched his lips. 'It would require the doing of certain things that can't now be done. It would be too risky by far. It's a shame you didn't think of creating a burglar or a mysterious stranger. They're always good and have often been used.'

'Well, come to think of it, it's quite futile to consider any of these things, for I've just remembered that Howard's mother called an hour or so ago, and I told her that I'd seen Howard and that he'd left me.'

'Damn it, Willie, it was damn inconsiderate of you to let me go on and on evaluating possibilities that were not possibilities at all.'

'I didn't mean to be inconsiderate. I simply forgot temporarily that she'd called, that's all. You're pretty touchy this morning, Quincy, if you ask me. I hope you're not going to take advantage of me just because I'm in trouble and need your help.'

'Not at all. I only ask you to understand that this kind of mental work calls for a special aptitude and is, moreover, considerably more exhausting than digging ditches. I don't appreciate being put to any unnecessary effort.'

'All right, all right. Mother Hogan called, and I'm sorry I didn't remember to tell you.'

'Good. Now that you've remembered, it's evident that there is only one thing to do. Howard must be disposed of.'

'That was my opinion from the start, but I couldn't think of any way to accomplish it. It's simply incredible, the problems involved in disposing of someone secretly. Do you have a suggestion?'

'I read an account once of a man who

reduced a friend to small pieces and put him in cold storage in neat little packages. Afterward he was able to dispose of him a package at a time. However, this would be messy and tedious and take up more time than I care to give to Howard. Besides, this man was caught, which doesn't speak well for the method.'

'Oh, do be sensible, Quincy. Surely you aren't serious.'

Quincy didn't answer. Perhaps he didn't hear. He got up and walked around the room, pinching his lip and looking at things with shining eyes. After a while he stopped beside Howard and inspected him for a moment thoughtfully, and then he moved back to the bed and sat down again.

'Of course, we might take him apart and ship him somewhere in a trunk or a large box, but the experience of others has shown the consequences of this to be inevitably disastrous.'

'Quincy, I simply will not tolerate taking Howard apart or reducing him to small pieces.'

'I see. Since he was your husband, I

suppose it's to be expected that you'd feel a certain amount of sentiment for him. It doesn't matter, anyhow, for I've decided what to do. You've told my stupid aunt that Howard left you. This was actually what Howard planned to do, as evidenced by the bag here on the bed and the two on the floor. Very well. We get rid of the bags and Howard together, and it is clear to all that the bounder has simply deserted. We must make the thing convincing, of course. We will have to manufacture a few more bits of evidence to support it.'

'Excuse me, Quincy, but I can't see that we are a bit ahead. We're still left with the problem of disposing of Howard.'

'True. I'm thinking about it. In spite of the temptation to do something unusual and elaborate, I think we had better make use of one of the tried and proven methods. Bodies, Cousin, are normally disposed of by cremation or burial. Since we do not have facilities for cremating old Howard, we must bury him. Nothing is needed for that except a spade and a small plot of ground.'

'What plot of ground exactly? We can hardly bury him in the back yard.'

'Leave it to me, Cousin. It so happens that I have an uncle on my mother's side who lives on a little farm southwest of town. I used to go swimming in the creek there when I was a kid. I still go out to see the old boy once in a while, as a matter of fact. He's a bachelor and a kind of bum and tells the most fabulous lies that you are expected to accept as gospel. There's a back way onto the farm, a little road around a cornfield and through a pasture to the creek. We can find a spot in there that will do nicely for Howard. I wouldn't mind being buried there myself, to tell the truth, if I had the misfortune to be dead.'

'Won't it be risky? Suppose we're caught.'

'After we get there, the risk will be negligible; and fortunately for us, this phony neighborhood you live in is made to order for such a venture. What with the big yards all cluttered up with trees and brush and stuff like that, we should be able to get Howard out of here without anyone but us the wiser. We simply load him in your station wagon in the garage and haul him off. It will have to be done late tonight, I think. Old Howard won't stay sweet much longer.'

'Do you honestly think anyone will believe that Howard walked away and disappeared without a word to anyone?'

'As to that, it's our part to make it impossible to believe anything else. Old Howard was a nut in his own way, you know. I've heard him say myself that he intended to run away someday to the South Seas and live naked with the natives. He used to say it publicly every time he got loaded. One thing we must do is get rid of his new Buick. Is it in the garage?'

'Yes, it's there with the station wagon.'

'Good. Tonight, after burying Howard, I'll get rid of it. Then everyone will think he simply drove off in it.'

'Are you sure you're not trying to be a little too clever, Quincy? I've read that being too clever is the thing that generally trips one up in the end.'

'Well, I'm like Tom Sawyer in that

respect. If you're going to have an adventure, you may as well dress it up and make it worthwhile. Are you beginning to question my talent, Cousin?'

'I would only like to know how you propose to get rid of a Buick automobile. It was difficult enough to think of a way of disposing of Howard. After all, Quincy, an automobile is too big to bury.'

'In the disposal of the Buick, my mother's side of the family will come in handy again. I have a cousin in KC who has made a career of stealing automobiles. At the beginning of his career, he served three years at Jefferson City for it, but since then he has perfected his methods and has had no more serious problems. He has an established market for stolen automobiles, and I'm sure he'd do me the favor of stealing Howard's. All I need to do is slip it away from here in the dark and drive to KC and let this cousin know where he can pick it up. Naturally we'd have to allow him all the profit, but the service would be worth it. The Buick would be repainted and fixed up with phony papers and wind up getting sold in California or someplace like that.'

Willie stared at Quincy with overt admiration and gratitude. It was simply incredible, she thought, how such an ugly, burr-headed runt could be so diversified and talented. He was better at love than a Boccaccio monk, as she well knew, and here he was as cool and clever in a crisis as anyone could possibly be.

'I swear to God, Quincy,' she said, 'you're truly remarkable, and I don't mind saying so. You're literally full of good ideas, and you know helpful people of all kinds that no one would ever suspect you of knowing.'

'Most of them are relatives on my mother's side,' Quincy said. 'All in all, the Hogans are a dull tribe.'

She was slightly annoyed by his complacency, and the feeling of annoyance must have pricked her to a higher kind of criticism, for something immediately occurred to her that seemed such an egregious oversight on his part that it made her uneasy about everything else he had suggested.

'Quincy,' she said, 'it's all very well to make clever plans about disposing of Howard and the bags and the Buick, but who is going to believe that he would go off without making any financial arrangements whatever?'

She was quite proud of having thought of this, for it seemed to her a very important consideration, but Quincy was clearly not in the least impressed. His attitude of complacency became, if anything, somewhat more pronounced, and she could see that he had not overlooked the matter of finances at all, but obviously was holding something in reserve with respect to them.

'Cousin,' he said, 'this raises a point that may shake you up. My position at the bank has put me in possession of a bit of intelligence of which you are apparently ignorant. The fact is that old Howard, only yesterday, wiped out your joint savings account in the amount of $10,587.27, and cashed, at the same time, somewhat more than $9,000 worth of government bonds, face value, at least half of them matured.'

'What?' she said. 'What's that?'

'It's true. I didn't handle the transaction myself, but I made it my business to learn the facts.'

'Why in the world would he do such a thing? Do you suppose he's been gambling or something?'

'Howard? Fat chance. In my opinion, Cousin, old Howard was planning to do exactly what we are planning to make him appear to have done. Our little indiscretion last night may have caused him to advance his time of departure a few hours or days, but it was not really the precipitating factor at all. Old Howard was getting out in any event.'

'Well, what a damn dirty trick. I've never before heard of anything so deceitful in my life. Whoever would have thought Howard capable of such a deception?'

'You'd better be thankful that he was. As it is, our case is supported nicely, and you could hardly have picked a better time to do old Howard in if you had planned it deliberately.'

'It's easy enough for you to be

philosophical, Quincy. You can afford it, I suppose, since you haven't been deprived of almost $20,000.'

'Fortunately for you, old Howard was the kind of fathead who puts everything in the sort of husband-and-wife joint ownership that makes it possible for either to tap the till without the concurrence of the other. The twenty grand is legally as much yours as his. All you need to do is keep it.'

'I'd be happy to keep it if only I knew where to find it.'

'Well, that's a problem we should now apply ourselves to. First, I'll just have a look in old Howard's wallet. He certainly couldn't have all the money there, of course, but any part of it is at least a beginning.'

He went over and deftly explored pockets with light fingers. From the inside pocket of Howard's jacket he extracted the wallet, and from the wallet several crisp bills.

'Eight hundred,' he said, after counting. 'I judge that the rest is in the smaller of the packed bags on the floor.'

'So far as I can see,' Willie said, 'it might just as well be in the larger one.'

'No. Old Howard would have wanted to keep that much cash pretty close to hand. The smaller bag would be easier to lug about, and that's where he probably put it.'

He opened the bag, and there, sure enough, it was. It was in a heavy manila envelope, 9 x 12, and Quincy handed the envelope to Willie, together with the eight hundred, and closed the bag again.

'All this money!' Willie said. 'It's simply incredible that Howard intended playing me such a dirty trick.'

'Well, it hardly matters,' Quincy said, 'since it turned out in the end to be a favor. Incidentally, now that you have the money, it will be necessary for me to have about three hundred for expenses.'

'Expenses? Whatever for? I hope you aren't going to start blackmailing me, Quincy.'

'Don't be absurd, Cousin. What's the need for blackmail between two reasonable people who enjoy such amiable relations as you and I? I have to make a little trip, that's all, and I'll need to fly in order to save time. Since I'm doing it for your sake, you surely don't expect me to pay my own way.'

'I simply don't see the necessity for making a trip. Where are you going?'

'Dallas, Texas, I think, would be as good a place as any. Old Howard is going to send you a letter from there, Cousin, and under the circumstances, as you can see from examining Howard, I'll have to go down there and mail it for him.'

'It seems like a long way to go just to mail a letter.'

'A husband on the run, Cousin, could hardly write from the next town. I can leave KC tomorrow after arranging matters with my maternal cousin about the Buick, and with luck I should be back and safely in my cage at the bank by Monday morning. If I'm delayed and a little late, you can rely on me to make an acceptable excuse.'

Willie looked at him dubiously with a recurrence of the uneasy feeling. It seemed to her that he was enjoying himself a little too much, and he seemed determined to elaborate everything as much as possible. She did not object to his getting pleasure from his efforts, for he had surely earned it, but she didn't want him to come a cropper over his own cleverness. She would have felt a little easier in her mind, in fact, if he had not exuded such perfect self-confidence.

'You are welcome to the money,' she said, 'if you really think it essential to go.'

'Thanks, Cousin.' He took the money, three hundred dollars, and shoved it into a pocket as he walked to the door.

'I'll be back tonight. Ten o'clock or thereabouts. Be certain that there are no obstructions in the way of what must be done. In the meanwhile, I hardly think it's necessary to emphasize the importance of not letting anyone get a glimpse of old Howard there.'

'I'm not quite an idiot, Quincy,' she said indignantly. 'I can see the importance of that as clearly as you.'

6

After he was gone, the day stretched out forever. It would simply be impossible, she thought, to do nothing but sit around the house and wait for night to come and Quincy to come back, and so she began to think of things to do, and the first thing to do, she decided, was to dress. She locked the bathroom door from inside Howard's room, and then she left through the door into the hall, carefully not looking at Howard while she was leaving, and locked the hall door with a key from the outside. It would now be impossible for anyone to wander into the room, which would have been possible before, if unlikely, and she carried the key to her own room and put it into her little jewel box on the dressing table.

She then removed the thin blue gown and went into the bathroom and had a shower, hot and cold, and she had the queerest feeling, which was rather frightening, that the sound of the shower would surely waken Howard, and that he would be, if she were to open the door and look into his room, standing and yawning and scratching in the rather revolting way he always did after waking.

Because of this feeling, she did not stay in the shower as long as she would have otherwise. In her bedroom, after drying on a huge wooly towel, she dressed in a white jersey pullover blouse, a kind of T-shirt, and a pair of bright red Capri pants to match her toenails. She was trying her best to be cheerful and to look on the bright side of things; but in spite of her best efforts she kept feeling more and more depressed, and even the considerable amount of money she had acquired, or salvaged, thanks to Quincy, was not enough to leaven her depression appreciably.

She took the money out of the envelope and counted it, but it was no use; it did not help much at the moment. She put it back into the envelope, and the envelope into a drawer of her dressing table.

She began thinking about what to do next, and she remembered all at once the little gun with which she'd shot Howard. She had carried it into the room with her last night, and there it was on the table by the bed. It would be wise to clean it and put it away, or perhaps even wiser to dispose of it entirely. The more she thought about it, the more she was convinced that the latter would indeed be the wiser. The safest thing to do, she thought, would be to bury the gun with Howard that night, although there really didn't seem to be any reason why the gun should ever become an issue if it was never known that Howard had been shot. Nevertheless, it was just as well to be as careful as possible and to anticipate contingencies. It would not be necessary, in any event, to do anything about the gun until it was time to do something about Howard; and this was certainly a relief, for it was something she didn't relish doing.

The truth was, the presence of Howard was becoming oppressive. Being so close, just beyond the bathroom, he persisted in being thought of, and she was constantly aware of him lying in there on the floor with his muscular proteins coagulating. Or were they, by this time, un-coagulating? Well, either way, coagulating or un-coagulating, Howard's muscular proteins were not pleasant to think about. She wished that it were possible to remove Howard from the house immediately, instead of tonight; but it wasn't, of course, for obvious reasons. The next best thing would be to remove herself, which *was* possible. She began to think about going somewhere, and where, specifically, she could go.

While considering this, Willie went downstairs into the kitchen and got some ice out of the refrigerator and carried it in a little pink plastic bucket into the living room. She put some of the ice into a mixing glass, which she took from a liquor cabinet, and added four parts of gin to one part of vermouth. She stirred this briefly with a glass rod, and it came out as a big Martini, which she began to drink slowly a small sip at a time.

The Martini was refreshing — an important quality of Martinis in general — and she was feeling much better when the telephone began to ring. Carrying the

Martini, she went out into the hall and answered the telephone. It was Mother Hogan again.

'Willie,' Mother Hogan said, 'has Howard returned yet?'

'No,' Willie said, 'he hasn't.'

'Have you made any effort to find out where he went?'

'No, I haven't.'

'I must say that you seem strangely indifferent.'

'Well, he took three bags with him, and so I assume that he went quite a long way to stay quite a long while.'

'What I want to know, Willie, is what you did to drive poor Howard away.'

'I didn't do anything to him. He simply packed and left after saying the nastiest kind of things that were all untrue.'

'What things exactly?'

'Never mind, I don't care to repeat them.'

'Howard has been very fair all his life, even as a small boy; and it's my opinion that he must have had a good reason for saying anything he said.'

'You may think as you please about it,

but I have a splitting headache, and I prefer not to discuss it with you.'

'Don't think you can avoid your responsibilities, Willie. Honestly, you have not turned out a bit better than I thought you would. It seems to me that you have been treated exceedingly well for a girl with little to offer in return, and the least you could do is show a little appreciation and the proper concern for Howard. It would serve you right if he didn't come back at all.'

'As to that,' Willie said, 'I'm not at all sure that he will; and I'm not sure, either, that I give a damn if he doesn't.'

Mother Hogan whinnied and hung up with a bang, and Willie hung up afterward and drank what was left of her Martini and went back into the living room to see if there was any left in the mixing glass. There was some left, all right, and she poured it and drank it.

She was feeling better because of the Martini, and better still because of having told off Mother Hogan, who had it coming to her, the fat bitch. And she began to wonder if she should mix some more gin and vermouth in the mixing glass, or if she should instead call some-one, a friend, and arrange for lunch downtown. If she went downtown, however, she would have to change clothes, which would be a bother; and besides, she couldn't think of any friend she particularly wanted to meet.

For another thing, she would have to open the garage door to back the station wagon out, and it was possible that someone might come by at that moment and see the Buick in the garage, where it was parked. That would spoil Quincy's plan to get rid of the Buick quietly and pretend that Howard had driven away in it. Willie felt quite proud of herself for having thought of that — the possible consequences of opening the garage door, even for a minute or two — and it showed, she thought, that she was self-possessed and almost as clever as Quincy himself.

It was a bright, sunny day outside, as she could see through the living room windows; but it didn't look very hot, and it was apparent from the way the leaves of the trees were moving that there was a breeze from the southwest. She thought that it might be pleasant to sit on the back terrace for a while, especially if she had another Martini or two to drink while sitting, and so she mixed some more gin and vermouth and went out the back way to the terrace, carrying the mixing glass in one hand and her cocktail glass in the other.

She sat in a striped canvas chair under a striped umbrella, and she had sat there long enough to drink one whole Martini slowly when she thought she saw a flash of movement and color through the leaves of the high hedge that separated the Hogan yard from the yard of the house next door, which was the house owned and occupied by Marvin and Gwendolyn Festerwauld.

Willie stood up and walked over to the hedge, about fifty feet, and peeked through. It was Gwen over there on the other side. She was lying on her stomach in the sun on a yellow pad, nearly naked in nothing but a couple of scraps of white. Gwen thought she had a superior and exciting figure, and she went nearly naked at every opportunity, but Willie didn't think Gwen's figure was really exceptional at all; and as a matter of fact, it was rather ridiculously exaggerated in places. It had to be admitted that men seemed to find Gwen's figure exciting, and Willie had heard comments to that effect from various sources; but then, of course, men were inclined to find almost anything exciting if it was nearly naked.

Anyhow, regardless of her figure, Gwen was someone to talk to at the moment, and someone to talk to was what Willie was beginning to want and need. Besides, it would be an opportunity to develop the deception that Howard had gone away last night after coming home from the club, and it was important to have that idea spread and accepted as widely as widely as possible in view of the fact that Howard was certainly gone and certainly wasn't coming back and would have to be satisfactorily explained.

Again feeling proud because she was thinking so clearly and was contributing her share to the successful execution of

Quincy's plan, Willie walked down along the hedge and around it and up into the Festerwaulds' yard where Gwen was lying. 'Hello, Gwen,' she said.

Gwen rolled over and sat up, leaving the upper scrap of white lying detached on the yellow pad. Picking up the scrap, she held it casually in front of the place it was supposed to go. Her eyes were foggy and did not seem to focus properly, and the skin beneath the eyes had a bruised and baggy look. She looked, altogether, like a bad day after a hard night.

'Oh, it's you, Willie,' she said. 'How are you?'

'Considering everything, I'm pretty well. And you?'

'Well, considering everything, I feel damn lucky to be alive. Or do I? Perhaps I'd be better off dead.'

'Why don't you try a very cold Martini?'

'Jesus, Willie, do you want me to die immediately?'

'Nothing of the sort. It would make you feel much better. I've had two or three myself, and I'm as good as ever. I'll mix you one if you like.'

'No, thanks. I prefer to recover, if I must, in my own way. What I need is about eighteen straight hours of sleep, but it's impossible to sleep at all while my damn head is simply bursting.'

She fell back and folded an arm over her eyes, and Willie sat down Indian fashion on the pad beside her. Marvin and Gwen had been at the impromptu party at the club last night, and Marvin had certainly been feeling his oats, as well as other things, some of which belonged to Willie. Willie had danced with him several times and could personally testify to this.

'Did the party go on for long last night after I left?' Willie said.

'It didn't last long at the club,' Gwen said, 'but it moved on somewhere else and lasted for hours.'

'Where did you go?'

'I don't remember clearly, but it was someplace outside of town on the high-way. There were some rough characters there who kept making snide remarks, and finally Gus Wilhite challenged one of them to a fight. They went outside and knocked each other around a little, and this seemed to clear the air and satisfy everybody, for after that everything was all right. I danced several times with a fellow who said he drove a truck for someone or other, and he wanted me to leave with him and go somewhere else, but of course I couldn't, with Marv there and all, and I can see, now that I'm sober, that it was for the best. God, Willie, it's simply incredible what one will do when one has had a few too many drinks.'

'Yes, it is. It's also incredible who one will do it with.'

'God, yes. Imagine a truck driver, if you can!'

'Were you tempted to leave with him?'

'I was tempted, but fortunately, as I said, I couldn't.'

'How did Gus come out?'

'Gus? Come out of what?'

'Well, Gwen, you just said he challenged a rough fellow to a fight, and they went outside and knocked each other around.'

'Oh, that. Gus came out all right. He

received a small cut at the corner of his mouth and possibly a loose tooth, but he wasn't especially concerned. Gus is tough, you know. He keeps in good shape by spending almost all his time swimming and playing golf and tennis.'

'What time did you get home?'

'I haven't the faintest idea, except that it was getting daylight. By that time I merely wanted to fall right over dead in bed, but Marv was getting sober and mean, as he always does, and he absolutely insisted on picking foolish quarrels and shouting at me at the top of his voice. Did you by any chance hear him?'

'No.'

'Well, with all the windows closed because of air conditioning, I don't suppose you could. Anyhow, he kept quarreling and making silly accusations concerning me and certain other men, and after an hour or so he took a cold shower and dressed and went downstairs, but by then he had succeeded in keeping me awake until my head was bursting, and it was no longer possible to sleep. I tried and tried for ages, but I couldn't, and so I finally put on my bikini and came down here to lie in the sun.'

'What's become of Marv?'

'Oh, he had this eight o'clock appointment at his office with someone about something. It was important, he said, so he had to keep it. When he left he was feeling pretty sick and subdued, no longer inclined at all to shout and make accusations. I really felt rather sorry for the poor bastard, to tell the truth, but of course it's insane to waste any sympathy on him. After his appointment is over, he'll close his office and go to sleep and come home later, about five or so, as if he had behaved all along with perfect decency.'

Willie sighed and shifted her position, hugging her knees beneath her chin. 'You're fortunate,' she said, 'that matters will be settled so easily between you. As for me, it seems that I've been left for good.'

Gwen unfolded her arm and sat up again abruptly. The movement must have caused her considerable distress, for she winced and closed her eyes and pressed the heels of her hands against her temples. After a moment, she shuddered and opened her eyes and stared at Willie with all the curiosity her condition permitted. 'What did you say? Been left?'

'That's what I said.'

'By Howard, you mean?'

'Of course by Howard. Who else, I'd like to know, could I be left by? Your mind is certainly not working well today, Gwen, if you don't mind my saying so.'

'If it were working like a watch, Willie, I'd still find it difficult to believe that Howard would do anything so decisive. No doubt he's only bluffing and will be home soon.'

'I wish I could think so, but I can't.'

'Come off it, Willie. You know very well that Howard is incapable of going through with it.'

'You think so? Maybe you don't know Howard as well as you believe. He was always talking about walking off from everything and going somewhere to some island or something for the rest of his life.'

'Oh, I've heard him say such things myself, but I'm sure it didn't mean anything. As a matter of fact, Marv talks like that sometimes, the idiot, but I don't pay any attention to it. All husbands have such fancies, darling. They like to imagine themselves lying around on a beach drinking fermented coconut juice and diddling native girls night and day. It's part of being a husband.'

'It's kind of you to try to reassure me, Gwen, but I'm convinced that it's much more serious in Howard's case. He packed three bags and left and has been gone without a word ever since.'

'Since when?'

'Since right after I got home from the club last night. You may remember that he came home ahead without me, and I was forced to catch a ride with his cousin Quincy.'

'I remember. But why did he pack and leave? Damn it, Willie, even a husband doesn't go off like that for no reason at all. What did you do to cause it?'

'It wasn't anything I did. It was merely something he thought.'

'Please don't be evasive, Willie. What did he think?'

'He thought I'd been outside doing something with Quincy. His own cousin, Gwen! Can you imagine?'

'Yes, I can, as a matter of fact. I've had experience with cousins myself, Willie, and I know what some of them are capable of. However, on second thought, I'm prepared to make an exception for Quincy. Cousin or not, he's quite unthinkable as a person to go outside and do something with.'

'Oh, I don't know. Quincy's all right. You'll have to admit that he's exceptionally clever.'

'What on earth does being clever have to do with it? In the matter of choosing someone to do something with that would be likely to make a husband leave you, cleverness has no significance at all that I can see. Are you defending Quincy, by the way?'

'Why should I? It's no matter to me what you think of him.'

'You did seem to be a little sensitive.'

Willie stood up and smoothed her

Capri pants over her hips and looked bored. 'I thought I could depend on you to be sensible, Gwen, but apparently I can't. If you're going to be ridiculous, I don't believe I care to stay and talk with you any longer.'

'That's all right, Willie. I feel like hell, and it would suit me fine if you were to go away.'

'In that case,' Willie said, 'I'll go.'

She went back along the hedge and into her own yard. She was proud of the way she had spread the idea of Howard's desertion to Gwen beyond the hedge, who would certainly spread it a great deal further as soon as her head quit bursting. Now Willie thought that she would like to go inside and have a sandwich and another Martini and a long nap, and that's where she went and what she did.

7

In the meantime, as Willie did these things and spent the day, Quincy was happily engaged. He devoted himself to Willie's problem, now that he had permitted himself through sentiment to become involved, with genuine enthusiasm.

The truth was, he had always wanted to try his wits at something major that did not, at the same time, demand an excess of tedious labor. That had always been the difficulty with science and law and mathematics — any of the fields in which he might have excelled if he had chosen to apply himself. While certain elements tickled his brain, these elements always became so closely allied eventually with plain *work* that all the fun was taken out of them. It was a shame, really, that one couldn't build a rocket or devise a serum without going through unconscionable labor in doing so. It was much more pleasant, in the end, to do nothing much about anything.

Willie's problem, however, was much to his liking. The consequences of failure would be unfortunate to be sure, but the exhilaration of success would be enormous. Overall, the entire project should require only a short while, while the work involved would be exciting and different, and would not have time to pall and become tedious.

It would be necessary, first of all, to contact his cousin on his mother's side, Fred Honeyburg by name. It might, moreover, take some time to make this contact, for Fred was a restless sort, always moving about, and could only infrequently be found in his pad in KC.

After leaving Willie, therefore, Quincy had a late breakfast in the coffee shop of the Hotel Quivera and then drove immediately in his secondhand Plymouth to KC, a distance of about fifty miles, and through the city to Fred's pad, which was on the third floor of a building on Troost.

As he suspected, Fred was not there and had not been there, discernibly at least, according to the tenant of the pad adjoining, for some three days and nights.

Quincy was a little disturbed by the fear that Fred might have gotten himself into jail again, just when he was badly needed. But the fear was easily allayed, for Fred was really ingenious at avoiding jails, and had never, except for the one unfortunate incident related by Quincy to Willie, had any intimate experience with them.

Recalling Fred's favorite bar in the downtown area, Quincy drove there and went in. Luck was with him, as it usually was, for there was Fred, sure enough, sitting on a stool at the bar and drinking Schlitz and watching the game of the week on television. There was an empty stool beside him, which Quincy claimed. 'Hello, Cousin Fred,' he said.

Cousin Fred turned his head, looked at Quincy, immediately picked up his glass of Schlitz and drank deeply before answering, as if he expected a trying series of events to begin transpiring from this point and was preparing himself for them. 'Hello, Cousin Quincy,' he said cautiously. 'What brings you to town?'

'I came to see you, as a matter of fact.'

'Is that so? Why?'

'Let's move over to a table where we can talk confidentially.'

'Well, I don't know, Cousin Quincy. The last time we had a confidential talk it cost me a hundred skins.'

'Forget that. I've got a proposition that will get your hundred back and a lot more besides.'

'What's the pitch?'

'Damn it, Cousin Fred, I can't talk about it here. Let's move over to a table.'

Cousin Fred drained his glass and looked into it for a few seconds without speaking or moving. He obviously had an uneasy feeling that the series of events he had immediately anticipated at the sight of Quincy had almost immediately begun to happen. He had a notion that he should, if he were smart, extricate himself at the very beginning, but he had another notion that he wouldn't. Quincy was a compelling little bastard when he wanted to be, and was not above exploiting family loyalty if it became necessary.

'Let's take a couple of beers,' Cousin Fred said.

Quincy bought the beers, which were carried to a little table in a dark corner. The entire place was dark, so far as that went, for Cousin Fred was averse to light and preferred in his places of relaxation the soft comfort of shadows. Physically, he bore a superficial resemblance to Quincy, a common inheritance of certain attributes on the maternal side; but the resemblance was so thin that a third party would hardly have noticed it even if the light had been a great deal stronger than it was. Although they were of a size, rather under the average, Fred's features were sharper and his eyes had acquired a furtiveness from looking into corners and over his shoulder that Quincy's lacked. Quincy's eyes, as a matter of fact, had an open and childlike innocence that was quite appealing, although deceptive.

Fortified by another large swallow of beer, Cousin Fred said, 'Now, Cousin Quincy, let's hear the pitch.'

'What I want you to do,' Quincy said, 'is steal a car.'

'Cousin,' Fred said, 'I use the word *appropriate*.'

'I don't care what you call it, so long as you do it.'

'Well, you must excuse me if I seem a little dubious, but this is the first time in a long career that I've had anyone ask to have a set of wheels appropriated. Already, Cousin, there's something in this pitch I'm beginning not to like.'

'It's perfectly simple. I leave the wheels, as you say, in a place we shall agree upon. At a time that we shall also agree upon, you make the appropriation and drive away. The only stipulation is, you must dispose of the car immediately. The profit is all yours. I ask for nothing but your service, and I appeal to you because I know you are an expert in these matters and have a sound knowledge of the market.'

'Those wheels of yours, Cousin? The profit wouldn't pay for the effort.'

'Not mine.'

'Whose, then?'

'Never mind whose. The car, however, is a new Buick. The profit, even in your market, should be considerable.'

'I don't like it. You wouldn't be trying to fix me with some kind of rap, would you, Cousin?'

'The trouble with you, Fred, is that the nature of your work has made you unnaturally suspicious. Would I play a dirty trick like that on the only son of my own mother's sister?'

'Yes.'

'Well, let it go. I guarantee that there's no risk to you whatever. The fact of the matter is, I'd be in far worse trouble than you if you were caught, which is a condition I naturally want to avoid.'

'Now I get you, Cousin. Now I'm ready to believe. Why do you want these particular wheels appropriated?'

'The less you know about that, the better. I tell you there's no risk and all profit.'

Cousin Fred drank beer and stared moodily at the thin foam on what was left. He couldn't rid himself entirely of his uneasy feeling; but at the same time, like any businessman, he was tempted by a clear profit quickly acquired, and he was pretty certain now that this was part of a larger matter that Quincy could hardly afford to play fast and loose in. It was quite clearly something that Quincy wanted done quickly and expertly with no chance of detection.

'When do you want the wheels appropriated?' he said.

'Sometime early in the morning. After four o'clock, say.'

'Where will they be parked?'

'My idea is to leave the car in the municipal parking lot. I'll leave the key in the ignition and the parking ticket in the glove compartment. All you'll have to do is pay the parking fee and drive away. All perfectly overt and innocent. The attendant who takes your stub when you leave will be different from the one who gives me the ticket when I arrive, and so there's no chance of arousing suspicion there. It's doubtful that anyone would pay any particular attention to either of us, anyhow.'

'True, Cousin. I like the sound of it. It's solid.'

'Do you agree to do it, then?'

'For the sake of our dear old mothers, I do.'

'Good. I knew I could count on the family tie.' Quincy drained his glass and stood up. 'Any time after four, but you better hadn't make it too long.'

'I get you. My market stays open all hours.'

'Goodbye, Cousin Fred.'

'Goodbye, Cousin Quincy.'

Quincy went outside and back to his Plymouth. He was confident that Cousin Fred would dispose of the Buick expertly and expeditiously; he felt no concern about that. The problem would be, of course, to get it out of Howard's garage and out of Quivera without detection; but this should also, because of the detached and woody character of the neighborhood, be accomplished without untoward incident. He had no less confidence in his own cleverness than in Fred's.

In the Plymouth, he drove north across the Sixth Street Traffic way to the Municipal Airport. He parked the Plymouth and went inside and inquired at an airlines desk about flights to Dallas, Texas. He was not in the least surprised to learn that there was an available seat on a plane leaving early the next morning, but not so early that he couldn't catch it after completing his necessary tasks. He was not surprised because he had that feeling of quiet elation which comes with the assurance that everything is going right, just right, and the feeling was even more secured by the information that he could catch a plane back that would land him in ICC tomorrow night, the night of the same day of his departure.

He bought a round-trip ticket in the name of Elton E. Smallwood and went back to the Plymouth and started home. There remained, of course, the small risk that someone from Quivera who knew him might be on the same plane to Dallas. Citizens of Quivera were not flying out of the airport every day, however, or even a substantial percentage of days, and so the risk was hardly a material danger; and it only added, even if it was, a little salt to the sauce. He did not question his capacity to handle the situation if it developed.

There was now the letter to think about, and he thought about it earnestly on the way to Quivera. He felt that a husband's farewell letter to his deserted wife, written at the beginning of a great adventure, between one life and another, should have the quality of artistic excellence. He felt, moreover, that he was just the fellow to achieve the quality, but he was handicapped by Howard's limitations. Unfortunately, in spite of a certain shrewdness in certain matters, Howard had been barely literate. It would never do to give the letter the polish it deserved, for then no one would ever believe that old Howard had written it. He would have to be satisfied, Quincy thought, with achieving a clumsy intensity — a kind of appropriate lubberly pathos. And this, to be sure, would be challenge enough to ingenuity.

The letter would have to be typewritten, of course. He could not, even if he had time to practice, which he didn't, duplicate Howard's scrawl. He wondered for a moment if it would be readily accepted that such a personal letter would he written on a typewriter, and he decided that in Howard's case it would. It was well known by nearly everyone that old Howard, because his writing was practically illegible, wrote everything on a typewriter, hunt-and-peck style. He had a Royal portable in his bedroom at home, as a matter of fact, and this would have to be disposed of, along with Howard and the three bags, to support the deception that he had taken it with him and had used it in Dallas to write the letter. There was almost no chance that there would be any sample of the machine's typing about, for Howard never wrote anything important enough for anyone to keep; and even if there were, it wouldn't really matter, for there was also almost no chance, the way matters were going so smoothly, that any investigation or comparison would ever be made. Still, for perfection's sake, the letter must be written on Howard's machine. What he would do, Quincy thought, was write it out in longhand this afternoon and then type it tonight when he went to Willie's.

Back in Quivera, he had lunch in the

hotel coffee shop and a couple of beers afterward in the hotel taproom. While drinking the beers, he carried on a lively conversation with the bartender, who was a frustrated philosopher; and when he left he was, consequently, in a cheerful and creative frame of mind. He went immediately to his small apartment and began to compose on plain paper, sitting at a table by a window overlooking the front yard and the street, the letter from Howard to Willie. He enjoyed the task so hugely that he was tempted to write pages, but he was compelled by the character of Howard to reject the temptation. It was certain that Howard had never in his life subjected himself to the ordeal of writing more than a few lines at a time, and so Quincy, now Howard's proxy, kept the letter short and the words small and the punctuation restricted to capitals and full stops. When he was finished, he read what he had written with satisfaction:

DEAR WILLIE:
I'm gone and I won't be back. Don't try to find me because you can't and

even if you could I wouldn't come back anyhow. I drew out all the money in the savings account and cashed all the government bonds but you can have everything else and welcome except the Buick which I'm driving.

I know what you thought. I know what everyone thought. You and everyone thought I was just a kind of good natured common guy who didn't ever want to be anyone or anything but someone around Quivera, but you were all wrong. All my life ever since I was a kid I've had a secret notion to run off somewhere a long way off and live the way I want to and now I'm going and gone forever. Maybe I'll paint pictures or something like Gauguin.

I'm not mad at you. I'm not mad at anyone. If this makes you unhappy or causes you any trouble I'm sorry but I've got a notion you won't miss me much. If you want to do me a favor you can tell Mother and Father goodbye for me. I didn't see them before I left because I was afraid I'd get weak and not go.

Goodbye forever,
        HOWARD

After reading the letter over, Quincy struck out the line about maybe painting pictures like Gauguin. He considered it extremely unlikely that Howard had ever heard of Gauguin.

8

He walked to Willie's, carrying a bag with a change of clothing in it, and he got there about ten o'clock. Willie, who was waiting for him downstairs in the living room, opened the door at once.

'Quincy,' she said, 'where in hell have you been?'

'This morning,' he said, 'I went to KC to make arrangements with my Cousin Fred about the Buick, but I've been home since the middle of the afternoon. Why?'

'I've been waiting and waiting for you.'

'Well, there's nothing we can do until it becomes sufficiently late, so I didn't think there was any particular hurry.'

'At least you could have come and kept me company.'

'Under the circumstances, I think we had better be a little cautious about keeping each other company for a while, don't you?'

'No one else has been here at all. It

wouldn't have made the slightest difference if you'd come.'

'That's true, as we now know, but you'll have to admit that we couldn't have anticipated it. You're inclined to be emotional in situations where you should be detached. It's a damn good thing, in my opinion, that you have me to help you.'

'You're a darling to be so helpful, Quincy, and I admit it. It was just that I kept being lonesome and wanted you to come, but now that you're here everything is all right again.'

He sniffed the odor of juniper berries and inspected her closely. He had not been aware of anything unusual about her at first; but now, clued by the odor, he saw that her eyes were a little foggy, and that her small face had assumed a kind of sultry laxness, and that she was in fact about half-shot on what was probably Martinis.

'Something tells me,' he said, 'that you've been drinking.'

'I've been drinking a little, it's true, but not excessively. I've only had a few Martinis because I was lonesome and needed them.'

'Please do me the favor of not having any more for any reason until we have disposed of Howard. It will be a difficult job at best, and we'll need to be in good condition for it.'

'We? I was hoping you'd be able to accomplish it without my help.'

'No chance. I'm rather small, as you can see, and Howard must weigh two hundred at least. Dead weight. I'm afraid I couldn't possibly lug him about by myself.'

'All right, I'll help if I must. It's only fair to do my part.'

'I'm glad you see it that way, since nothing would otherwise be done at all. What have you been doing all day?'

'This morning I went next door and talked with Gwen Festerwauld, and then I came home about noon and had a nap, and since then I've merely been doing this and that and having a few Martinis and waiting and waiting.'

'What did you talk with Gwen about?'

'I told her that Howard had left me, because I thought it would be a good idea to get the story started around, and there's no one who can get a story started around any better than Gwen.'

'That's true. It's just as well to get people talking about old Howard's desertion as quickly as possible, and Gwen's just the one to do it. I congratulate you, cousin.'

'I am only doing my part. What do you have in the bag you have set there on the floor?'

'A change of clothing. I'll certainly need a bath, too, when we return from disposing of Howard. Lugging him about, in addition to digging a hole for him, will be hot and dirty work. I also have a pair of cotton gloves in my pocket, incidentally. It's very rare that I do anything to get blisters on my hands, and someone might consider it curious if I suddenly turned up with some.'

'I swear, Quincy, you simply think of everything. You're about as clever as one person can be. Did you say you went to KC?'

'Yes.'

'And arranged about the Buick?'

'Yes. I'll drive it over there after we're

through with old Howard.'

'Do you think your cousin can be trusted?'

'Don't worry about Fred. Discretion is essential in his business, and he's the soul of it. Now I think it's time we got busy. The disposal of Howard will take considerable time, and then I must change clothes and drive the Buick to KC for Fred to appropriate, and afterward catch a plane to Dallas, Texas.'

'Are you actually going to Dallas to mail a letter?'

'Certainly. Can you think of any other way to get it mailed that wouldn't be too risky? Don't worry, Cousin. I'll be back tomorrow night and safely in my cage Monday morning. The modern miracle of transportation, you know. I've written the letter, incidentally, and the first thing I must do now is type it on Howard's portable Royal in his room. We'll dispose of the portable with the bags and Howard. Come along upstairs. After I've typed the letter, you may read it and give me your opinion.'

'I don't believe I care to read it. It

would surely make me sad.'

'Never mind. You'll read it soon enough when you get it in the mail.'

They went upstairs, Willie leading. Quincy waited in the hall outside the door to Howard's room while Willie went into her own room and got the key and returned with it. Now that he had completed the necessary preliminaries to the disposal of Howard, Quincy was excited and satisfied and eager to get on with the principal business. He hummed a little tune under his breath as he waited. When Willie returned and let him in, he went directly to Howard and leaned over him for a moment and then straightened again with a pleased look.

'Fortunately,' he said, 'old Howard bled very little, and the position he assumed in falling has prevented him from dripping on the carpet.'

'Quincy,' Willie said, 'I'd appreciate it if you wouldn't insist on trying to discuss such details with me. You'll make me positively ill if you aren't careful.'

'I'm not trying to discuss it. I only mentioned it as something that must be considered. Where is Howard's portable?'

'He kept it in the closet, I think. You'll probably find it pushed back on the floor.'

'All right. While I'm typing the letter, you can make yourself useful by carrying down the bags and putting them into the station wagon in the garage. The back seat must be folded down, of course. Is there a spade in the garage?'

'There's a spade and a rake and some other tools.'

'The spade will be sufficient. We'll need a flashlight or a lantern, however.'

'There's no lantern that I know of, but there's a flashlight already in the glove compartment of the wagon. Howard always kept it there in case of a flat tire or something at night.'

'That was very accommodating of Howard, I must say. Well, you take care of the things I've mentioned, and I'll get on with the letter.'

He went over to the closet and found the portable where Willie had said he probably would. Although he was proficient in the touch method, he typed the letter hunt-and-peck out of deference to

Howard. He typed it on plain paper, which he had brought with him; and after it was finished with appropriate strike-overs, a Howard-ish touch, he typed Willie's name and address on a plain envelope and put the letter into the envelope and sealed it. By that time Willie had returned, slightly disheveled and panting a little from her labors.

'Quincy,' she said, 'I'm bound to say it's damn inconsiderate of you to make me do all the hard work while you simply sit and peck at a typewriter.'

'Please don't complain, Cousin. You've only done a few necessary things, while I've completed something important that required my personal attention. Besides, I'll have my share of hard work before we're finished. Now, I think, it's time to carry old Howard down and put him in the station wagon.'

'I wish it could be avoided.'

'Obviously it can't, unless you want me to drop him out the window and load him from the lawn.'

'Oh, well, I don't think I want you to do that. Besides showing disrespect, it might attract attention if someone happened by.'

'In that case, as I said, we must carry him down without any further delay.' Quincy went over and prodded Howard gently with a toe and then reached down and pinched his cheek. 'Old Howard's mighty stiff yet. He'll be very difficult to handle. Damn it, Willie, why didn't you think to turn off the air-conditioner in here today?'

'Would that have made a difference?'

'Certainly it would have made a difference. Surely you can understand the basic principle of cold storage. However, it's too late now, and we will have to do the best we can with Howard as he is. Take hold of his feet, Cousin, I'll give you the advantage of the lighter end.'

Willie did as she was told, and took hold of his feet; but it was clear that it required an enormous exertion of will, and that she would have greatly preferred not to. Quincy, at the head end, backed across the room and out into the hall, Howard between and Willie following. And it was perfectly true, as Quincy had predicted, that Howard was extremely difficult to handle, besides being very heavy; he seemed to have a perverse determination, in fact, to go in all directions except the one in which he was being guided.

At the head of the stairs, Quincy and Willie rested a few seconds, catching their breath for the descent. Then they started down, Quincy still ahead and bearing the brunt of the weight as it naturally took on a momentum of its own in his direction. Willie was aware that Quincy had arranged this deliberately out of consideration for her, and she was sorry that she had complained about having to load the bags and the spade.

They were about halfway downstairs and going along very well, in spite of Howard's perverseness, when a bell began to ring suddenly, which was rather disconcerting, to say the least. They stopped, put Howard down and listened; and it turned out to be, as they had both feared, the bell at the front door.

'Well,' Willie said, 'if this isn't the worst kind of imposition. All day long no one has come at all, not a single person, and now all of a sudden here is someone at the door just when he couldn't be less welcome.'

'Who do you suppose it is?' Quincy said.

'I haven't the least idea. Do you think I should go down and find out?'

'Perhaps you should. We can't afford to take the chance that it may be someone who will hang about outside if there's no answer.'

Willie walked around Howard and Quincy and down the stairs and the hall to the door, which she opened a crack to see and talk through. Quincy listened intently, but could not hear what Willie was saying, or what was said to her; but he hoped that it was judicious on Willie's part, whatever it was. And it must have been, he was relieved to note, for she closed the door shortly and came back to the foot of the stairs.

'It was only a man asking where the Bowsers live,' she said. 'Fortunately, it's in the next block, and he's gone down there. I was afraid for a moment that it might be

Mother Hogan come to see if Howard had returned.'

'It's high time, in my opinion, that Howard was *leaving*. Turn off the lights in the hall and the living room, Cousin. We'll have to do the best we can in the dark.'

Willie turned off the lights and came back and took up her end of Howard, Quincy doing the same with his end, and they got the rest of the way downstairs and back through the hall and into the kitchen to the door leading directly into the garage.

The darkness added to their difficulties, but they arrived without accident, except that Quincy backed into the corner of a cabinet and cursed a little, and Howard was bumped sharply against the jamb of the kitchen-garage door. Howard did not curse or care, of course, and a minute later he was deposited safely in the wagon beside the bags and the spade. Quincy went back upstairs for the typewriter and was down again in another minute.

'Now we must back the wagon out and get started,' he said. 'You go outside through the small door, Cousin, and be certain that no one is passing when I open the big one. It would spoil things if the Buick were seen by someone who might remember it.'

Willie followed directions, knocking on the big door from outside to indicate that the coast was clear, and Quincy quickly opened the door and backed out the wagon and closed the door again. When he resumed his seat behind the wheel, Willie was beside him.

It did not matter if the wagon was seen, since it was not supposed to be gone, and so Quincy turned on the lights and backed out of the drive in a normal way. Driving down Ouichita Road in the direction away from town, he was shortly on a gravel road, and shortly thereafter on a dirt road that would take them along the back limit of his maternal uncle's farm.

The road was deserted and the night was dark: all aspects of the venture, he thought, were favorable. The bumping of Howard among the bags and the spade made a comfortable kind of sound in his ears. 'You'll have to admit,' he said, 'that everything has gone admirably under my direction.'

'I do admit it,' Willie said, 'and I only wish I could think of an adequate way to express my appreciation.'

'Well,' he said, 'perhaps later we can think of something.'

They came to a turn-off and stopped after turning. Quincy got out and opened a section of barbed-wire fence that served as a gate. Willie drove through the opening onto a narrow track, no more than a trace of wheels between a cornfield and a high hedge of Osage orange. After resuming his place behind the wheel, Quincy drove down along the hedge slowly to the end, where it was necessary to repeat the process of opening a section of fence, and from there quite a long way across an open pasture to a stand of timber along a creek. He stopped the wagon in the dense darkness beside the trees.

'The spot I have in mind,' he said, 'is just across the creek, and it will be necessary to walk from here. The water isn't very deep in this place, but the bank on the other side is quite steep.'

'Couldn't we do it on this side just as well?'

'The other side is better for our purpose. For one thing, it is less likely that someone will come poking about over there before the last signs of old Howard's last abode have been obliterated by nature. For another, the bank is higher and excludes the chance of a disastrous wash in case the creek rises. Lastly, the ground is softer and spades easier. Come along, Cousin. Remember that I'm working on a tight schedule.'

He removed the flashlight from the glove compartment and shoved it into a side pocket of his jacket. Moving around to the rear of the wagon, he opened the tailgate and pulled Howard out onto the ground. He had the impression that old Howard had limbered up a little on the ride out.

'First things first,' he said. 'I'll have to return for the bags and the portable and the spade. Positions as before, Cousin. Watch your step in crossing the creek. The water will be hardly above your knees, but the rocks underfoot are slippery.'

His voice and entire attitude were a little too cheerful to suit Willie, who was becoming rather depressed again, not to say apprehensive. But she supposed that she must concede him the right to take a certain pleasure in the successful execution of his plans. He had already taken Howard under the arms, so she took up the feet again, and they moved off in the same order as before, he leading and she following and Howard, naturally, between. The ground was rough and treacherous, but the creek bank was fortunately low on this side, no steep decline to the water, and they got safely down without mishap and into the water and about halfway across before anything unfortunate occurred. Then Willie inadvertently stepped down on the side of a round rock and lost her balance and fell with a splash. Howard, released at the nether end, swung downstream with the current and was only prevented from floating away by the determined resistance of Quincy. Willie got up, gasping and soaked, her blouse and Capri pants plastered to her body. The night air felt suddenly twenty degrees cooler.

'Kindly be a little more careful,' Quincy said. 'Can you imagine our position if old Howard had got away from me? It would be absolutely impossible to find him in the water in the darkness.'

'Well,' Willie said indignantly, 'I have never before heard anything so unfair. Here I've fallen into the water and gotten soaked, and might even have broken a leg or something, and all you can do is be cross and critical. I'm doing my very best, Quincy, and that's all that can be expected of me.'

'Oh, well, never mind. No harm has been done. At the worst you've only wet your pants.'

'Please don't be vulgar, Quincy. I'm hardly in the humor for it.'

'Excuse me. I'm only trying to keep your spirits up. I'd appreciate it, Cousin, if you'd resume your position. Old Howard's pulling like the devil to get away, and I'm becoming slightly tired.'

Willie found Howard's feet beneath the water and took them up again, and the crossing was completed. The bank on the other side, however, was a problem. It was about six feet high and very steep, almost vertical, and it was plainly impossible to walk right up it, let alone with Howard between. They leaned Howard against the bank in a semi-upright position while Quincy considered the matter. 'I'll have to haul him up from above,' he said. 'Hold him in position until I can clamber up, and be certain that you don't let him fall forward into the water and get away.'

'Don't worry, Quincy. I'm perfectly capable of holding Howard until you're ready.'

She proved it by doing it, and Howard was hauled up safely by Quincy. Willie clambered up afterward, and it was from there only a hundred feet or so downstream to the spot Quincy had chosen. Willie was forced to concede that it seemed a very likely spot. It was among a cluster of bramble bushes where someone would go infrequently, hardly ever, and the chances of Howard's being discovered were satisfactorily negligible. After resting a minute or two, Quincy prepared to return to the wagon.

'You had better stay here with Howard,' he said. 'I'll be back in a few minutes with the things.'

'Perhaps I'd better go with you. You'll surely need help carrying them.'

'No. After all, we must now do old Howard the courtesy of keeping him company until he is properly disposed of. I'll have to make two trips across the creek. You can come down to the crossing on this side and help from there.'

'Well, please hurry, if you will. I don't feel inclined to stay here with Howard indefinitely.'

She was feeling rather uneasy, as a matter of fact. The instant Quincy was gone, the night was filled with a thousand sounds that had not been there before. The worst of the sounds was the crying of an owl somewhere among the trees, and she had a notion it was watching her and taking Howard's part against her. She wished it would stop crying and fly away, but it did neither, and there was no way to make it.

After a bit, she walked down the bank and found the spade and two bags,

Quincy obviously having gone back for the rest. She carried the bags and the spade back to the cluster of bramble bushes, and pretty soon Quincy came along with another bag and the portable. The owl kept crying, but Quincy didn't seem to hear it; or if he did, didn't mind.

'I'll require a little light now,' Quincy said. 'Here is the flashlight. Keep it pointed at the ground and shielded as much as possible above. It's almost certain that no one will come around to see it, but it's just as well to be cautious.'

She sat down beside Howard and held the light, and Quincy got to work with the spade. He seemed to be quite strong for a little guy who was generally allergic to physical exercise, and he worked along steadily with infrequent brief breaks for rest. Once, as a kind of token courtesy and to show her willingness to do her part, Willie offered to dig a little in his place; but he declined, as she expected, and it was pleasantly surprising, all in all, how quickly the time began to pass and how soon an adequate hole was dug. It would have been dug even sooner if it hadn't been necessary to allow space for the bags and the portable that must also go in. Willie became so intrigued by Quincy's demonstration of unsuspected physical effectiveness that she actually forgot to listen to the owl; and when she finally remembered to listen again, it was gone, or at least silent.

'Well,' said Quincy, climbing up and out, 'it's now time to put old Howard in.'

'Yes,' said Willie, 'I guess it is.'

After he was in, Willie thought that it would only be proper to say something appropriate. She tried to think of something, but she couldn't think of anything original and couldn't remember anything prescribed for such occasions. Then Quincy, who was clever and could always be relied upon, put in the bags and the portable and said, 'Well, so long, old Howard. Drop us a line from Dallas.' This seemed enough to be said, and nothing remained but to cover him up and spread some twigs and leaves around.

They went back along the bank and across the creek, Quincy stopping to wash the spade in the water; and then, in the

wagon, back across the pasture and between the Osage orange and the corn to
the road.

'As I expected,' Quincy said, 'it went
well.'

9

This was the night, of all the nights it might have happened, that Cousin Fred met Fidelity Stemple. Heretofore, Cousin Fred's approach to women had been direct and simple, even somewhat primitive; and if the approach was no more than moderately effective on the whole, it had at least left him unfettered and uncluttered, free alike of uncomfortable commitments and emotional hangovers. If someone would, she would. If someone wouldn't, she wouldn't. And if she wouldn't, to hell with her. That, in brief, was Cousin Fred's position.

Or had been. Before this particular night, that is: the night Quincy and Willie disposed of Howard, and Cousin Fred met Fidelity. At first, of course, Cousin Fred didn't know if Fidelity would come across or not. But he had immediately a miserable feeling that it was an issue of greatest importance that could not be dismissed, that if she wouldn't, assuredly she would with someone else.

Cousin Fred had been walking down this dark street at about midnight, and suddenly he was listening to one of the most remarkable passages of profanity he had ever been privileged to hear. He stopped and continued to listen with proper admiration, at the same time peering ahead to locate the source; and there was this slim little young woman with a pale ponytail standing on the sidewalk ahead of him. She was standing spread-legged with her arms akimbo and her fists on her hips, and leaning far forward from the waist to look into the dark interior of a set of parked wheels. A Caddy. It was apparent that someone in the interior was the subject of her invective, and Cousin Fred's first judgment was that he'd better get the hell out of there before the fight started; but he didn't know whether to slip on past in the direction he was going, or to turn and retreat in the direction from which he had come. In the moment of indecision, the profanity came to an abrupt halt, and he was aware that the girl had straightened and turned and was watching him in what appeared to be an attitude of friendliness.

'The son of a bitch is drunk,' she said with apparent good humor.

'Is he?' Cousin Fred said cautiously.

'Stinko, the slob. Come here and see.'

Cousin Fred approached and peered into the Caddy. A fat man was sprawled in the front seat with his head fallen back and his mouth open in a carp-like expression. His heavy breathing had the sound of gargling, but his breath didn't smell like Listerine.

'Stinko, all right,' Cousin Fred conceded. 'That's plain enough.'

'We were in that little bar around the corner,' she said, 'and he kept drinking all those goddamn boilermakers, just to show what a hell of a man he was. No sooner did I get him outside, after trying for hours, than he began to puke, and he puked all over himself. Can you smell him, sweetie? Go on and smell the slob.'

'I smell him.'

'Well, it's not the smell of roses, is it? I hope to God I die if I ever go out with another fat guy as long as I live, even if he's got a million dollars. I never went out with a fat man in my life who didn't turn out to be a slob one way or another.'

What Cousin Fred couldn't understand was why this girl had felt compelled to go out with any slob whatever, fat or otherwise, for she was in his opinion by all odds the neatest girl he had ever encountered in KC, and could probably have had her choice of almost any guy you'd be likely to find up and down Twelfth around the clock.

'Why did you go?' he said.

'Go where, sweetie?'

'Out with this fat guy.'

'Because he has money, of course. Why else?'

'Do you like fat guys with money?'

'Well, I sure as hell don't like them *without* money.'

'Couldn't you find a guy with money who wasn't fat?'

'Oh, sometimes I do, of course,' she said thoughtfully. 'But it's rather astonishing, when you come to think of it, how many guys with money are fat. Besides, to be fair, they're inclined to be especially generous. There are certainly advantages to fat guys, if you can only stand their being such slobs. The problem now, however, is how the hell I'm going to get home.'

'Can't you drive?'

'No, I can't. Isn't it ridiculous? I'm probably the last woman alive who can't drive an automobile. I can't understand it myself really, but the moment I try, I head immediately for the nearest building or pole or whatever solid is handy. Do you suppose you could possibly drive me home?'

'I don't have my car with me.'

'We could use this one. After all, the son of a bitch is obliged to get me home, isn't he? I'll tell you what. We could drive out most of the way and leave him in the car and walk on to my place and have a couple of drinks or something.'

This was a proposition that seemed to Cousin Fred to have interesting potential. It was almost four hours before he was supposed to appropriate the Buick for Cousin Quincy, and he couldn't, offhand, think of any way to spend them that had half the appeal.

The truth was, something strange was happening in Fred's gnarled little heart. And what was happening, although he didn't understand it yet, was something that had happened because of Fidelity to quite a few other men in much the same way. She looked almost statutorily young, standing there with her head cocked and the pale ponytail sticking up from it at a sharp angle; but the truth was that she had never been young at all. She had only, once, been an ancient child.

'Let's get the slob in the back seat,' Cousin Fred said.

He hauled the fat man out onto the pavement and then heaved him into the back seat while Fidelity, as her contribution to the effort, held the door open. Then they got in the front seat, Fred under the wheel, and he drove, following her directions, in a southeasterly direction that brought them in somewhat over twenty minutes to a respectable street on which, at intervals, there were respectable apartment buildings. During this time, names were exchanged and a rapport established.

'I live down on the next block, sweetie,' Fidelity said, 'but I think we'd better leave fatso here and walk the rest of the way. I don't want to litter the neighborhood with him.'

Cousin Fred pulled up at the curb, and they got out, leaving the keys in the ignition and the victim of boilermakers in the back, where he had fallen over onto his side on the seat, his knees drawn up against his belly in the posture of a gross and obscene embryo with prenatal gland trouble. He drew his breath loudly through his nose and expelled it through his lips, making bubbles.

'Looks like he'll sleep till morning,' Cousin Fred said.

'For all I care,' Fidelity said, 'the son of a bitch can sleep forever. Come on, sweetie. I'll fix you a nice Hi-Fi Special for your trouble.'

'What's a Hi-Fi Special?' Cousin Fred asked warily.

'It's a drink I made up myself out of brandy and rum and vodka and some other stuff. You'll like it. You see how I got the name? Hi is the way it makes you, and Fi is for me, my name, because I made it up. You see? I use it on guys to make them generous, and you'd be surprised how it works. It's very effective, I mean.'

Cousin Fred, of course, had already decided what he wanted for his trouble, and it surely wasn't any lousy Hi-Fi Special. But he wasn't averse, nevertheless, to a preliminary social period, even one compounded of rum and brandy and vodka and stuff. Besides, if the recipe incited generosity in the hearts of guys, it would quite likely incite the same in the hearts of girls, including Fidelity, which would be a development well worth a hangover. His thoughts, though scatological, were qualified by tenderness, and he was beset by a strange uneasiness that he couldn't diagnose. He was merely vaguely aware that Fidelity might somehow become, if he wasn't careful — or even if he was — a threat to his emotional stability and his natural conservatism.

On the next block, they turned into her apartment building and went up to her apartment. It was obvious from the environment, which was comfortable if not luxurious, that she had indeed been the recipient of generosity which had certainly not all been inspired by Hi-Fi Specials only. He remarked on this with a faint accent of bitterness.

'Sweetie,' she said, 'it's just that guys seem to enjoy giving me things.'

'I'll bet they do.'

'It's true. They seem to get the greatest pleasure from it.'

'I don't doubt it for a second. I'll just bet they get the greatest pleasure, all right. I wouldn't mind getting some of that pleasure myself.'

'Well, you mustn't be nasty about it, sweetie. You surely wouldn't expect me to ruin a good thing by being chintzy with a guy who is being generous. Anyhow, as you know, it's none of your goddamn business.'

This terse reminder brought Cousin Fred up short. She was perfectly right, and he was bound to admit that he was acting like nothing but a lousy monogamist. Worse than that, he was thinking and feeling like one. Entirely, moreover, without justification. He had only met this girl, and here he was already, in less than an hour, wanting unreasonably to deny her the natural right to sleep around in her own best interests. He watched her moodily as she busied herself with bottles and glasses. Her straight little back was turned to him, and he observed her with a disturbing sense of attachment. After a minute or two, she brought him a tall glass containing a vile-looking liquid with a couple of ice cubes floating in it. He took a long swallow of the liquid while she stood with her head cocked, the pale ponytail sticking up at any angle behind, to observe his reaction. And it was to his credit that his reaction was restrained.

The mixture of brandy and rum and vodka and stuff was only waiting for the catalytic action of his stomach juices to set it off like a bomb. After the detonation, he hung onto the glass with both hands as if it were a lamppost while his organs settled into place and his head stopped spinning.

'What do you think of it?' she said.

'I've never tasted anything quite like it before,' he said

'Of course you haven't. It's my secret recipe. You can't buy it at a bar.'

She raised her own glass to her pink lips and tipped it. She had apparently developed a tolerance for Hi-Fi Specials, for there was no discernible effect. Cousin Fred, watching her, was overwhelmed by a feeling of fuzzy admiration. Setting his glass carefully on a handy table, he grabbed her and kissed her fervently, but she had also apparently developed a tolerance for kisses. She accepted this one with good humor but with no warmth and no response.

'You mustn't get excited, sweetie,' she said.

'Let me stay the night,' he said.

'No, sweetie. It's impossible.'

'Why?'

'It wouldn't be right.'

'You've let others stay.'

'It was different with others. I had good reasons, sweetie.'

'What reasons?'

'They gave me things or money for the

rent or something. It wouldn't be right to let you stay just for fun.'

'By God, I never heard anything so crazy in my life before.'

'It's not crazy to have principles, sweetie.'

'All right, all right. I'll give you something for the rent.'

'You don't look like you could give me enough to make it worthwhile, sweetie. I don't want to hurt your feelings or anything, but you don't look very rich.'

'You might be surprised.'

'I don't think so, sweetie. I've developed an instinct about such matters.'

'Oh, come on, Fi. Let me stay.'

'No, no, sweetie. I'm sorry, but it's a matter of principle.'

'Goddamn it, you'd have let that fat slob stay if he hadn't passed out. You know you would.'

'Well, he's a big real-estate dealer from out of town, and he was going to take me on a little trip for a few days.'

'Where?'

'Never mind where. It doesn't matter, since he surely won't take me now, the son of a bitch. I was looking forward to it, as a matter of fact. I'm sick of this town and need a change.'

'If I were to take you somewhere, would you stay with me?'

'Sleep with you, you mean?'

'You know damn well that's what I mean.'

'Of course, sweetie. It would only be fair. You mustn't start getting excited again, however, for I'm sure there's no place you could afford to take me that I'd want to go.'

'Don't be so sure of that. How would you like to go and spend a week in a fine lodge on a lake and not have anything to do except swim and lie in the sun and go boating and out dining and dancing at night and things like that?'

'It sounds heavenly, sweetie, but you mustn't tell me any lies, because I'm far too experienced in these matters to give you anything in advance on account.'

'I'm not asking for anything in advance. I'm asking you to go with me first and find out for yourself that I'm not such a lousy bum as you seem to think.'

'Could it be that you're serious?'

'Damn it, I am! Will you go?'

'How will we get there?'

'We'll go in my car, which is a new Buick Roadmaster.'

'Honest to God, do you really have a fine lodge on a lake and a new Buick Roadmaster?'

'I said I did, and I do. You'll see.'

'I admit that I hardly believe it. I was certain that you were poor, sweetie. When would you like to leave?'

'Well, I loaned the Buick to a friend, but he's going to return it by four o'clock at the latest.'

'In that case, I'd like to leave as soon after four as possible. It's God's truth that this town has become so depressing that I can hardly stand it. What you had better do is leave now and go get your Buick, wherever it may be, and come back for me as soon as possible. I'm sorry I thought you were hardly more than a bum. What you should try to do, sweetie, is cultivate a more impressive appearance. It's probable that you miss out on a lot of nice things by looking so unimpressive.'

'Sure,' he said with some asperity. 'I ought to be a fat slob, that's what I ought to be.'

'Well,' she said, 'you mustn't lose your temper and spoil things, now that we have reached an understanding and matters are looking pleasant for both of us. If you have a long way to go for your Buick, you had better call a taxi from here, for it might be difficult to find one on the streets at this hour.'

He called the taxi and went down to the street to wait for it. He knew that he was behaving recklessly, and he felt a proportionate uneasiness, but it was absolutely clear that Fidelity wouldn't in some circumstances and would in others; and he was determined, at whatever risk, to establish the circumstances in which she would. Anyhow, he thought, the risk surely wasn't great. Old Quincy had said as much, and it was pretty certain that Quincy wouldn't be involved in something like the appropriation of wheels, which was out of Quincy's line, if he hadn't assured himself ahead of time that there was practically no chance of anybody getting caught. It surely would do no harm to delay the delivery of the Buick a few days or a week, especially since it would be, in the meanwhile, down in the sticks by the lake he had mentioned, where it would hardly be seen, or attract any attention if it was.

There really was a lake and a lodge. The lodge didn't belong to Cousin Fred, of course, but he couldn't see that it would hurt anyone if he simply borrowed the use of it. It actually belonged to the man who operated the market for appropriated wheels with which Cousin Fred did business. Cousin Fred frequently did various errands for this man, who was a man of some importance, and one of these errands had taken Fred to the lodge on the lake. Being a perceptive fellow, he had recognized at once the possibilities of such a place, and he had seized the opportunity of having a duplicate made of the key with which he had been entrusted.

It certainly paid to think ahead, he thought, sitting back in the seat of the taxi that took him downtown.

10

After he had bathed and changed, putting his soiled garments into the bag from which he took the clean ones, Quincy left in the Buick. Stealth being necessary, he and Willie had pushed it out of the garage onto the incline of the drive, and Quincy had leaped in nimbly and rolled backward to Ouichita Road without lights or engine. On the road, he swung upgrade backward and then downgrade forward, still without lights or engine, and disappeared silently behind the high shrubs and bushes that grew along the way.

Standing and listening in the drive outside the garage, Willie thought that she heard, finally, the Buick's engine come to life at least a block or two away. Then she went into the garage, closing the big door after herself, and up through the house to her own room. She saw by the little clock on her dressing table that time had moved far into the morning, and she wondered if Quincy would make it to KC on schedule. But she was not particularly concerned about it, for such matters could safely be left in Quincy's hands.

Fortunately for her, the exertions of the night had exhausted her, and sleep, she thought, would come quickly. She went into the bathroom and showered, abusing Quincy a little for the mess he had left. Then, in her bed, she lay and listened to the crying of an owl in her brain and went finally to sleep to the crying, although not so quickly as she had thought and hoped.

It was three o'clock the next afternoon when she opened her eyes and was instantly wide awake. It was clear to her at once that she was going to start thinking about things and getting depressed if she didn't do something to avoid it; and the first thing to do, as a beginning, was to leave the house and go somewhere else.

Considering places to go, she got up and walked over to a window and looked out onto the side lawn between the house and the hedge. And it was a hot day out there, filled with white sunlight. What she thought she would do then, seeing the hot white day, was to go swimming in the pool at the club. The muscles of her thighs and back and arms were quite stiff from the disposal of Howard, and the swimming would be therapeutic for them, as well as something to do for the sake of doing something.

She thought she would just wear her swimsuit under a beach coat. She put it on, which was rather a struggle because of its tight fit, and was on her way downstairs with the beach coat and a bright striped towel over her arm when the doorbell began to ring, and kept right on ringing imperiously. She was exorbitantly startled by the harsh sound, because it was a repetition of the incident that had happened last night when she was in practically the same position on the stairs — if not, fortunately, in the same circumstances.

She had thought then that it was Mother Hogan ringing, and she thought the same thing now, but then it hadn't been, and now it was. It *was* Mother Hogan.

The older woman came forcefully into the hall behind a magnificent bosom and stood looking sternly at Willie in her brief swimsuit. It was more of a glare than a look, to be precise. Mother Hogan, it was plain, was in no mood to tolerate equivocations. 'Willie,' she said, 'where are you going naked?'

'I'm not naked. I'm wearing my swimsuit, as you can see. It should be perfectly obvious, consequently, that I'm going swimming.'

'Shame on you, Willie! You're as nearly naked as it's possible to be publicly without being arrested. In my opinion it shows extremely poor taste to go about in that condition when poor Howard has disappeared without a word to anyone.'

'He didn't disappear without a word. He said a great many words that he damn well may be sorry for, and I'm determined that he must at least apologize for saying them when he returns, if he ever does.'

'Whatever he said, he must have been justified. Moreover, Willie, I believe that you know exactly where he went and where he is now. You're refusing to tell me out of spite, and I demand that you tell me the truth at once.'

'Go ahead and demand as much as you please. I've told you that I don't know, and I don't. It's true, however, that I probably wouldn't tell you if I did.'

'You see? You're a spiteful creature, Willie, and probably worse. Have you been carrying on some disgusting affair with someone?'

'I don't believe I care to discuss my affairs with you, disgusting or otherwise, and you had better be careful what you say unless you want to be sued for slander or something. It's well known that you're one of the worst scandalmongers in town, and care nothing whatever for the truth.'

Mother Hogan began to swell in the area of the bosom, which was already swollen enough, and to turn a kind of pale lavender in the face. Willie watched her uneasily in the fear that there might suddenly be another Hogan to dispose of, which would have made one more than she could possibly stand, and two too many. Mother Hogan wouldn't breathe, that was the alarming thing. She simply stood there and kept swelling and swelling and turning that odd lavender in the face and refusing absolutely to breathe.

Finally, however, just when it seemed that she must surely burst, she merely deflated instead in a kind of hissing anticlimax, like a punctured inner tube. 'Willie,' she said, 'you're a wicked girl to talk that way to a mother who is worried to distraction about her only son. However, I refuse to engage in further acrimonies. What I want to know is, do you propose to be reasonable and help me find Howard, or not?'

'No, I don't. Let Howard take care of himself. He has run away with three bags and the Buick and what else I don't know, and he can come back when he gets ready, if he ever does; but I'm not sure at all that I give a damn if he doesn't.'

'Very well. Now I understand clearly how you feel, and I must say it's not surprising in one with your background. I'll tell you something, though. There's something very odd in all this, including your attitude; and if I haven't heard from Howard by tomorrow morning at the latest, I shall certainly consult the police.'

'I wish you would. I'd like to consult them myself, as a matter of fact. I'm almost certain there must be some kind of law against desertion. It's probable that I have all kinds of rights and advantages I'm not fully aware of.'

Mother Hogan retreated, an affronted and quivering mass of indignation, and Willie waited until she had completely cleared the area before going to the garage and backing out the station wagon. She was somewhat disturbed by the threatened consultation with the police, and she would have to be quite careful about what she said if it actually became necessary to say anything. It might be rather difficult to explain things satisfactorily to someone inclined by his position to be suspicious; but then, on second thought, it probably wouldn't be so difficult after all, for she should have in tomorrow's mail, or Tuesday's at the latest, the letter from Dallas that Quincy had gone to send. As a matter of fact,

Quincy was certainly in Dallas at this moment, if he wasn't actually on his way back, and it was a comfort to think of him and how clever and helpful he was.

It was the practice of some people to consider Quincy a kind of failure, if not a joke; but it was certain that some of them who thought they were most superior — someone like Evan Spooner, or others she could mention — would have been no help at all in a critical situation like this, and in fact they couldn't even have been trusted to try.

There were quite a few members sitting at round tables on the terrace of the club, and there were a great many others out on the golf course playing golf, but there didn't appear to be so many out there as actually were, because they were so widely dispersed.

In the pool were mostly kids, jumping off the high and low boards and floating about on little inflated rafts and things, but there were a few women stretched out in the sun around the sides on bright enormous towels, and one of the women stretched out was Gwen Festerwauld. She was stretched out on her belly with her face buried in the crook of an arm; and Willie, who did not at the moment care to talk with Gwen, went past her and dove into the blue water that was not really blue at all but only looked so because that was the color the tank was painted.

The water was warm and deliciously sensuous on Willie's skin. She swam slowly across the pool and back a few times, avoiding the kids, and then lay floating on her back with her eyes closed. The warm, sensuous water was like a poultice, drawing the soreness from her arms and back and thighs. After a while, she rolled over and swam to the side and crawled out and spread her towel beside Gwen's and lay down.

Gwen lifted her head, screwing up her eyes in the bright light. 'Hello, Willie,' she said. 'Is it you?'

'Yes,' Willie said, 'it's me.'

'Would you mind telling me where you've been all day?'

'I've been at home, that's where. Why?'

'Because I was over at your house three times this morning, no less, and every time I rang and rang the bell but couldn't get an answer. Are you quite sure you were at home?'

'It isn't likely, Gwen, that I'd forget where I was just this morning. I was in bed and asleep all the time, and didn't get up until this afternoon, only a little while ago. I couldn't get to sleep last night, because of being upset about Howard and all, so I finally took some pills, and I guess I took more than I should have or something, since I slept so long and couldn't be wakened. Did you want to see me about something special?'

'I wanted to see if Howard had come back, that's all.'

'Well, he hasn't. Mother Hogan has been after me and after me to find out where he went, but I don't know and I don't care. He can come back or not. It's all the same to me.'

'Do you suppose anything could have happened to him?'

'Oh, nonsense, Gwen. If anything had happened to him, an accident or anything like that, I would have heard about it long ago. Men carry all sorts of identification about with them in their wallets and places.'

'That's true. It isn't likely anything has happened to him, I guess. You're probably right in refusing to get excited and behave foolishly. I told Marv about it, and he only laughed. He said Howard is sure to come back pretty soon.'

Gwen rolled over onto her back and shuddered. 'God, what a head! It's simply bursting.'

'Aren't you rid of your hangover yet? I must say it's the longest one I've ever heard of.'

'Oh, I'm rid of the one I had yesterday. This is a new one. As I predicted, Marv came home about five and was feeling chipper as you please and acting so positively innocent that you'd never have suspected him of being a perfect bastard only a little while before. He insisted on going out to a backyard barbecue that a friend of his had invited us to, so we went, and there were two large kegs of beer that everyone felt compelled to empty, which we did. I hope to die if I ever go to such a party again. It's really amazing, Willie, how everyone simply sheds all their inhibitions at a backyard barbecue with beer. It was all your chastity was worth to walk near a bush; and I can tell Marv, if he cares to know, that this particular friend of his who had the party has some very liberal notions regarding the prerogatives of friends.'

Willie buried her face in the crook of an elbow and quit listening. She was rather bored with Gwen's hangovers and imperiled chastity, the latter of which was a fiction anyhow. Lying in the therapeutic sun, she began to wonder what she would do with the rest of the day and the coming night, which might be a bad time if she did nothing to prevent it. What she planned to do was to go on lying in the sun for quite a long time and then swim some more in the warm water, which would feel cool after the sun, and finally to have something to eat and drink on the terrace, a sandwich and a salad and several Martinis. After that it would be dark, and she would drive home and take the pills that she had not needed or taken last night — or early this morning, rather.

And almost the next thing she would know, with luck, it would be tomorrow — another day that could be lived when it came.

11

The pills, as it turned out, were effective. Nine hours after taking them, she was wakened by the first-floor activity of Mrs. Tweedy, who had returned to duty after a two-day leave. Mrs. Tweedy, an ample woman of Irish extraction, did not so much approach her work as attack it. It always astonished Willie a little to see order and cleanliness restored under her hands, for it seemed from the accompanying clatter and thumping that she was, on the contrary, tearing the place apart. This excessive noise was generally annoying, especially early in the morning; but this particular morning it had exactly the opposite effect and was, in fact, as comforting to Willie as music or a warm bath. It seemed to signify the resumption of normalcy in a reasonable world where one could expect to survive comfortably, with a little luck and ingenuity, in spite of unexpected and unfortunate episodes that might disrupt events temporarily.

She climbed out of bed immediately and bathed and dressed and went downstairs briskly. Mrs. Tweedy was in the sunny dining room, and she received Willie with a moist eye and a determined cheeriness that informed Willie at once that the Tweedy ears had intercepted already the report of Howard's desertion. Well, there was no doubt where Mrs. Tweedy's sympathy lay. She had been herself deserted by two husbands, one who had thoughtlessly died and another who had thoughtfully caught a freight train going west; and even if she had known the true disposition of Howard, it is doubtful that she would have felt that he had received any worse than he deserved.

'Good morning, dearie,' Mrs. Tweedy said warmly.

'Good morning, Mrs. Tweedy. I believe I'll have a simply enormous breakfast, if you don't mind. Scrambled eggs and bacon and toast and jelly and coffee and a large glass of orange juice to begin with.'

Mrs. Tweedy was clearly nonplussed by this ravenous light-heartedness. She had been prepared to find Willie in distress, if not collapse, and she didn't now know what to say or what attitude to assume with this unexpected person who came downstairs demanding scrambled eggs and appeared to have been relieved of a burden rather than to have suffered a loss. For a moment, truth to tell, Mrs. Tweedy resented Willie's unwarranted behavior, which deprived her of the chance to play the faithful servant in a tight little domestic drama. But then she began to understand, of course, that Willie was only hiding her shame and hurt beneath a precarious pretension, the gutsy little thing, and it was enough to break your heart to see it. So much courage to find, Mrs. Tweedy thought, in one so slight — hardly bigger than a pound of soap.

Quickly adjusted and still moist of eye, Mrs. Tweedy retreated to the kitchen and returned with orange juice. Willie accepted it and began to sip it, sitting alone at the table in the morning sunlight. *What*, she thought, while Mrs. Tweedy cracked an egg in the kitchen, *shall I do today? One thing I must do*, she thought, *is see Quincy* as soon as possible and assure myself that everything went well with him on the trip to Dallas. This can be arranged easily enough, for all I have to do is go into the bank and cash a check at his cage, which will be a natural way to see him that will excite no suspicion. And fortunately I can still cash a check as an excuse for going, for Howard at least left the money in our joint checking account, the deceptive bastard, although he wiped out the savings account and cashed the bonds.

The bank will open at nine o'clock, and it is now past eight, so I will drive down there in the station wagon after I have finished my breakfast. I do hope everything has been completed satisfactorily with regard to the Buick and the letter — and I really have no doubt that everything has, for Quincy is exceedingly competent when he tries to be, and I have great confidence in him.

Mrs. Tweedy, after a while, returned with the rest of breakfast — golden eggs and crisp toast and coffee. Watching Willie devour these good things with apparently keen appetite, she admired more than ever the quality of Willie's pretension. You would never know to watch her, poor little thing, that she had suffered a great blow to her pride, if nothing else, and was holding herself together only with the greatest effort. Mrs. Tweedy did wish, however, that there was a way to refer to Howard's desertion in a natural manner that might elicit some discussion of the matter and afford her an opportunity to express her opinion, which was a decided one.

'Do you wish to speak with me about something, Mrs. Tweedy?' Willie said.

'I was just wondering if you might have some special instructions this morning,' Mrs. Tweedy said.

'No, I can't think of anything special.'

'About the cleaning, I mean.'

'There's not a great deal of cleaning to be done. Just the routine things.'

'What I mean is, should I clean Mr. Hogan's room?'

Willie was silent for a few moments, staring into the bright sunlight. Mrs. Tweedy thought that she looked very young and sad, like an unhappy child. It was apparent that the mention of Mr. Hogan's name — which wasn't, in Mrs. Tweedy's opinion, even the beginning of what he ought to be called — had upset her so greatly that she now must wait to regain control of her emotions before answering.

This was Mrs. Tweedy's interpretation of the silence, but it was not quite a true one. The truth was, Willie was trying carefully to remember if anything incriminating or suspicious might be left in Howard's room that Mrs. Tweedy shouldn't see. But she couldn't think of anything of that kind that had ever been there at all, except the gun and Howard himself, both of which had been removed. So after the few moments of silence, she nodded her head and said to Mrs. Tweedy that she should, of course, clean Howard's room as usual.

'You're a brave, sweet girl, dearie,' Mrs. Tweedy said.

After this oblique reference, Mrs. Tweedy went back to her work, wishing for Howard a fate almost as unfortunate as the one he had in fact suffered, and Willie finished her eggs and bacon and toast and poured a second cup of coffee from the pot on the table. She sipped the coffee and saw, looking out the window onto the side lawn, that Marv Fester-wauld's dachshund, Lester, had slipped through the hedge again and had treed the red squirrel that lived in a maple outside the kitchen door. It was plain from the ridiculous way in which he kept jumping into the air and opening and closing his mouth that Lester was barking at the squirrel, which was, no doubt — although he could not be seen by Willie — sitting on a branch above and chattering back at Lester. All of this absurd activity took place in perfect silence, because of the windows being closed for air conditioning, and this was what made it amusing and worth watching.

It made Willie think of the old question about whether a falling tree would actually make any sound if there were no one around to hear it. She had herself never cared for intellectual problems and discussions of that kind, not being the intellectual type; but it was something that would probably interest someone like

Quincy, who was always thinking about difficult things that didn't seem to matter much one way or another. It was time, she thought, now that Quincy had come into her mind in connection with Lester and the squirrel and the hypothetical falling tree, to go down to the bank and see if Quincy was all right and if everything had gone well with him.

She went out into the hall and called upstairs to Mrs. Tweedy that she was leaving, and then she went on to the garage and backed out the station wagon and drove down town. The large revolving clock attached to the bank building reported that it was nine fifty-three when she passed through the door below it, and the thermometer on the back side of the clock indicated eighty-six degrees. The instant she stepped into the cooled interior air, she had the most terrible and debilitating feeling that Quincy was not there in his cage where he was supposed to be, and that something disastrous had happened after all to spoil his plans and ruin everything.

The feeling was so strong, and her

conviction of disaster so certain, that she felt quite faint and could not force herself to look in the direction of Quincy's cage. Instead, she sat down on a wooden bench along the wall and stared at the floor until she was feeling normal again, except for the dreadful conviction of disaster. Finally, all at once in order to get it over with instantly, she looked up in the direction of the cage . . . and there was Quincy, safe and sound, in spite of her sudden foolish fear to the contrary.

She was seized by a wild compulsion to giggle aloud in sheer relief, but she buried the incipient giggle under a deep breath and stood up. It was just as well, as it turned out, that she had delayed on the bench, for Quincy was just finishing with a patron while the other tellers had been idle, which would have made it appear odd, to say the least, if she had waited for Quincy when there was no necessity. It just showed you, she thought, how even a bad experience could turn out for the better and be of service in the end.

She walked over to Quincy's cage and began to write a check to herself for fifty dollars, which she did not need, and Quincy smiled and nodded in a casual kind of way that was absolutely admirable, the cool and clever little devil. You couldn't possibly have told from observing him that they were any more than amiable cousins by marriage, or that either of them had been up to anything the least secretive or out of the ordinary.

'Good morning, Cousin,' Quincy said.

'Good morning,' she said. 'I'd like fifty dollars, if you please.'

She pushed the check through the little aperture, and Quincy asked her if she wanted it any particular way, meaning in particular denominations, She said no, and he counted out a twenty and two tens and a five and five ones.

'Did you have a good weekend?' he said.

'It was pretty quiet,' she said. 'Nothing much happened.'

'Same here.'

'It's going to be a hot day. I noticed by the thermometer when I came in that it's already close to ninety. I'll probably go swimming at the club later. About five.'

'Maybe I'll see you out there.'

Which meant that he would, and that was about all they could say — only casual remarks because of the chance of being overheard. But Quincy kept looking at her and smiling in that cool way of his, and just as she was turning to leave he slowly winked his offside eye in relation to the teller in the next cage, and she knew that everything had indeed gone well, as she had hoped and Quincy had promised.

Slipping the fifty dollars into her purse, smiling and nodding casually as one cousin-by-marriage to another, she turned and walked out of the bank. Her feeling of relief had grown into a kind of quiet elation and sense of well-being.

It was too early for lunch, especially after such a hearty breakfast, so she decided to spend some time shopping. She did this leisurely for about two hours, moving from shop to shop and leaving her purchases to be delivered or picked up later, for there was none among them that she really needed and very few, if any, that she would even want after she received them.

Shortly after noon she went to the Hotel Quivera and had lunch in the coffee shop. She wished she could have a Martini before and after, but the bar was not open yet. Lacking a Martini to linger over, she lingered instead over a glass of iced coffee, managing to kill another hour pleasantly before, on a kind of impulse, she went to a movie.

Sitting in the cinema, she remembered that she had failed to call Mrs. Tweedy and give notice that she wouldn't be home for lunch. This was a dereliction for which Mrs. Tweedy had practically no tolerance, and she would have to be pacified later.

The movie was exceedingly dull. The male lead was played by a young man whose hair was too long — longer, in fact, than that of the young woman who played the female lead, which was too short. In spite of being bored, Willie continued to sit in the cool, dark theater until her eyes happened to wander to the clock under a small light to the right of the screen, and she saw that it was half-past two. The time reminded her that the mail had surely been delivered on Ouichita Road, and that she might have a letter from Dallas.

Although there was no hurry to go and get the letter and read it, she nevertheless felt compelled to do so. She left the cinema and drove home in the station wagon, and there, still in the box, was the letter. It had come by air mail.

She carried it into the house and read it in the living room. In spite of expecting it and knowing all about it, she felt a strange and unpleasant little shock while reading it, as if it had actually been written by Howard himself, even though he was dead and buried among the brambles beside the creek on the farm of Quincy's maternal uncle.

As she stood there with the letter in her hand, feeling at first the shock and then a vague uneasiness, the bell at the front door began to ring. She went out into the hall and opened the door, not waiting for Mrs. Tweedy, who was upstairs.

A man was standing there with his hat in his hand. Willie didn't know him and couldn't remember having seen him before, but she had an immediate conviction that he was a policeman; and that was, in fact, what he was.

12

The Quivera police force included, besides a chief and the usual uniformed contingent, three plainclothes detectives, of whom one was Elgin Necessary, bearing the rank of lieutenant and presently standing at Willie Hogan's door with his hat in his hand. He was a tall, thin man with a tendency to droop at the joints, so that he gave an overall effect of being boneless and in the process of collapsing slowly with a whisper into a little pile of wilted seersucker. At this moment, as a matter of fact, he was rather embarrassed, and as a consequence rather angry. He felt that he was being forced to meddle without cause in something that was none of his goddamn business, and what he wished was that certain fat, nosy women in this town were not always imposing their nosiness on the goddamn police force in general and Lieutenant Elgin Necessary in particular.

He looked at Willie from under limp lids that never quite uncovered his eyes, in which there was now a gleam of appreciation. She was certainly a cute little trick, about a hundred pounds of a lonely man's dream, and he began to feel, before saying a word, like a lousy bully. 'Mrs. Hogan?' he said.

'Yes,' Willie said.

'I'm Lieutenant Elgin Necessary of the police. I'm sorry to bother you, but we've been asked to investigate the disappearance of your husband. Is it true that he's gone?'

'Yes, it's true, but it's a personal matter, and very unpleasant, and I don't see why it's necessary to make any investigation of it. Is it the custom of the police to make an investigation every time a husband runs away from home?'

'Only when there's a particular complaint or request. May I come in and talk with you about it?'

'I suppose, if you must.'

He went into the hall and followed her from there into the living room. He stood turning his straw hat by its brim in his hands, feeling now like a trespasser as well as a fool and a bully, until she had sat down on a sofa with her little stern just catching the edge and her knees together and her hands folded on her knees around what appeared to be a letter.

He also sat down, in a chair facing her, and dropped his hat on the floor.

'I imagine,' she said, 'that it was Mother Hogan who sent you here.'

'Mrs. Howard Hogan, Senior. She didn't really send me. She requested an investigation, and I was assigned. I'm sure we can get everything cleared up quickly with your cooperation.'

'I'm willing to cooperate in any way I can. What do you want to know?'

'Mrs. Hogan, your husband's mother, seems to be convinced that there is something wrong. Do you know why she feels that way?'

'She doesn't like me and merely wants to cause trouble for me.'

'You don't think it's anything more than that?'

'I don't know what more it could be. I've told her and told her that Howard and I had a quarrel. He went away with three bags that he was packing when I got home from the club, where we'd been to a party, and I haven't seen him since.'

'What time was this? When you had the quarrel, I mean?'

'I don't remember exactly, except that it was late. After one o'clock, I think.'

'Friday night?'

'Well, it was Saturday morning, to be exact.'

'Yes. Saturday morning after one o'clock. Did he leave the house soon after that?'

'Pretty soon. Maybe about two. He drove away in the Buick.'

'Did he give any indication of where he was going?'

'No, not then. I told Mother Hogan that he didn't, but she wouldn't believe me.'

'Did he take anything besides the three bags and the Buick?'

'Well, he had clothes and things in the bags, of course. I don't know what all. Clothes and toilet articles and things like that, I guess.'

'Do you know how much money he had on his person?'

'Yes, I do, the sneak. I didn't know it at the time, but I've learned today that he drew out all the money in our joint savings account, besides cashing all our government bonds, and altogether he had about twenty thousand dollars.'

Lieutenant Elgin Necessary could not repress a low whistle, and for a moment he gave the impression of being erect in his chair, although Willie could not remember afterward that he had actually moved discernibly at all.

'That's a lot of money,' he said. 'You're sure he had it on his person?'

'Of course I'm not sure. He'd hardly show it to me, after all, since he was running off with my share. He must have had it, though. Probably in one of the bags he packed.'

'With that much money, he must have planned to go somewhere to stay a while. He also must have planned in advance, as you must see. He evidently didn't leave solely because of your quarrel.'

'That's true. I can see it clearly, now

that I've learned about the money.'

'How did you learn about it? Did the bank notify you?'

'They didn't notify me, but I found out about it this morning when I went there to get a check cashed. Howard's cousin works in the bank, you know.'

'I didn't know, as a matter of fact.'

'He does. He works there as a teller. He was the one who told me about Howard's drawing out the money and cashing the bonds.'

'He did this on Friday?'

'Yes. Sometime Friday.'

Necessary looked down at his hands, which were lying in his lap. They were very large hands with knobby knuckles. One of them picked the other up and began to rub it with a massaging motion, as if it were in pain. 'Well,' he said, watching the performance of his hands, 'it seems pretty apparent that your husband planned to go away without your knowledge and that he made certain preparations in advance. Maybe he left a little earlier because of the quarrel, but he would have gone anyhow. That's the way it looks to me. Are you certain you can't think of where he might be?'

'Oh, I know where he is.'

He looked up from his hands, and again she had that queer impression of sudden sharp straightening of his body, although nothing actually moved except his head. On the contrary, he stopped the one small motion he was making, the one hand dropping the other and lying down quietly beside it in his lap.

'What's that? You know where he is?'

'Yes. He's in Dallas, Texas. At least he was there yesterday.'

'I thought you said you didn't know where he went?'

'I meant I didn't know where he went immediately after leaving, but now I know he's in Dallas, or was yesterday, because I received a letter from him in the after-noon mail.'

'Is that the letter you're holding?'

'Yes. I'd just finished reading it when you came. Would you care to see it?'

'It's none of my business, really. You needn't let me see it if you don't want to, but it would be kind if you would, and maybe it would definitely settle this business.'

'I want you to read it. You'll see that he has simply gone away and doesn't intend to return.'

He took the letter and read it with an odd feeling of reluctance and shame, as if he were committing in her presence some kind of obscenity. In order to read the typed words, he put on a pair of horn-rimmed glasses, which he took from the breast pocket of his seersucker coat. He looked, she thought, like a rather seedy high-school teacher who had probably once dreamed of becoming a scholar and moving up into a university, someplace like that, but had now resigned himself to being no more than he was, if not less. At the same time, however, he conveyed an impression of shrewdness that was brought into focus, like the words on the paper, by the glasses and the manner in which he peered through them.

After a couple of minutes, he returned the letter to her and the glasses to his pocket. 'Isn't it rather unusual to write a letter like this on a typewriter?' he said.

'Do you think so? Why?'

'It's a personal letter. Usually, it seems to me, such letters are written by hand.'

'That's so, of course, usually. Howard, however, never wrote anything at all by hand if he could avoid it. His handwriting was simply atrocious, hardly legible, and I think it embarrassed him. He had a kind of obsession or something about it. As you can see by the letter, he never even signed his own name unless it was on some kind of paper that required it.'

'Yes, I see. Where do you suppose he came upon a typewriter to use in this case? I mean, hotel and motel rooms are not equipped with typewriters, are they? When you come to think of it, a typewriter is not something that's readily available unless you have one of your own or know someone who will loan you one.'

'Howard had his own, of course. I told you that he never wrote anything by hand if he could avoid it.'

'Did he take it with him?'

'Yes. It was a Royal portable, and he had it when he left. I remember seeing it.'

'You said he took three bags. You mean

he took two bags and the portable typewriter?'

'No. I don't think so, now that I think about it. He took three bags and the portable.'

'Four pieces of luggage altogether?'

'Yes. That's right. Four.'

'I just wanted it clarified. You neglected to mention this before.'

'I didn't think it was particularly important. Is it?'

'No. It explains how he was able to type the letter, that's all.' Necessary stood up, started to cover his head with his straw hat and then, evidently remembering where he was, jerked it away and hid it behind his back. 'Thank you for helping me, Mrs. Hogan. You've been very considerate.'

'Not at all. I hope everything has been explained satisfactorily.'

'It seems clear enough. I'm sorry to have bothered you.'

'You are obligated to make investigations if they are requested, I suppose, however silly. May I offer you something before you go? A drink or something?'

'No, thank you. I'd better get along.'

He walked to the door ahead of her and turned there to say goodbye. He was reluctant to leave and would have liked to stay for the drink she had offered him. Although it was against regulations to drink while on duty, he had broken regulations before under lesser temptation. He didn't really know why he felt compelled to decline and leave. Perhaps it was because he was aware of a total inability to be detached in her presence. Talking to her and listening to her, watching her all the while as she sat primly with her small stern just catching the edge of the sofa, he had felt a strong impulse to take her in his arms and comfort her with kisses.

He had not felt like this in the presence of a girl, or a woman, for much longer than he cared to think about, and it disturbed him. It was far too late for such an emotion, almost adolescent in its poignancy; and it had been, in truth, always too late for him, even thirty years ago. Now, outside on the lawn, he yielded to another impulse, turning to wave to her as she stood in the doorway to watch him leave. She waved back and smiled, and he went on across the lawn to the drive and his car.

Driving downtown, he thought that it all seemed obvious, although a bit queer in spots. It was obvious that Mrs. Howard, Senior was a stupid and probably vindictive bitch who was getting excited about very little, which was what he had guessed in the beginning, and that Mrs. Hogan's son Howard had simply gathered up all available cash and deserted his wife, which made him in Necessary's book a damn fool who didn't know a good thing when he had it. Necessary was vastly relieved that the case could be closed so quietly and quickly — that there was, in fact, no case at all so far as he was concerned in his official position. He hoped, just as soon as he could get Mrs. Howard Hogan, Senior off his tail, that it would never be necessary to think of her again. But it would be quite a while, he conceded bleakly, before he would forget, case or no case, Mrs. Howard Hogan, Junior.

13

It was about five o'clock when the phone rang. Mrs. Tweedy, who was just leaving, answered in the downstairs hall. She called up the stairs to Willie, who was in her room getting ready to go out to the club to meet Quincy, and Willie took the call on the upstairs extension. 'Hello,' she said.

'Is this Mrs. Howard Hogan?' a voice asked.

It was a woman's voice, but it did not sound like the voice of any of Willie's friends or any voice that Willie had ever heard before. 'Yes,' Willie said, 'it is.'

'This is Gertrude Haversack speaking.'

'Oh?'

'I've called to ask you to come and see me.'

'I think you must have the wrong person. I'm Mrs. Howard Hogan, Junior. Perhaps you want Mrs. Howard Hogan, Senior.'

'No, not at all. You're the person I want, Mrs. Hogan.'

'Have we met before?'

'No, we haven't. You've probably seen me around town, but I doubt that you'd remember me.'

'In that case, why should I come and see you?'

'I think it's time we became acquainted.'

'Do you? That's very flattering, I'm sure, but I'm not so sure that I agree with you. Is there any particular reason why we should know each other?'

'I think so.'

'I'd be interested to know what it is.'

'Because I'm Howard's mistress. Or was.'

It was a sneaky and devastating verbal punch. Not the light jab that old Howard had actually been crawling into bed with someone named Gertrude Haversack, which was in Willie's opinion a minor aberrance that she could accept with no great sense of shock, but the thundering right cross of the changed tense. What did it mean? Did it mean only that Gertrude Haversack, whoever she was, had been

Howard's mistress but had now ceased to be for any one or more of the various reasons that women routinely cease to be mistresses or wives or whatever they were? Or did it mean, perhaps, that Gertrude had ceased necessarily to be a mistress because Howard had necessarily ceased to be a lover by reason of being dead and disposed of?

But this was not possible. It simply was not possible for anyone except Willie and Quincy to know the truth about Howard. Standing silently with the phone in her hand, thinking with a kind of fierce intensity in the sudden and thunderous roaring of the live wire between her and Gertrude Haversack, Willie needed considerably more than the sporting ten seconds to recover from the blow she had received.

Having recovered, however, she began to feel angry at Gertrude Haversack for playing such a damn dirty trick on her, even if inadvertently.

'Are you there?' Gertrude Haversack said.

'I am,' Willie said. 'I damn surely am.'

'Do you agree now that you should come and see me?'

'Why should I?'

'Because I have something to tell you that you will be interested to hear.'

'I don't think so. You are certainly a liar with something on your mind, although I can't imagine what it is; and if you have anything to tell me you had better tell it now, on the telephone, for I'm going to hang up if you don't.'

'You better hadn't.'

'Tell me whatever it is you have to tell.'

'Not on the telephone.'

'Goodbye, then.'

'You'll be sorry if you don't come.'

'Will I? Why?'

'Because if you don't, I'll have to go directly to the police.'

There was that sneaky punch again. Only this time Gertrude Haversack didn't even bother to set Willie up with a jab first, damn her. She just hauled off and threw the bomb without any preliminary.

Again Willie stood clutching the phone while the live wire roared in her ear, and it was a favorable reflection on her toughness that she was able to recover quickly from such an attack for the second time in as many minutes. 'What in the world do the police have to do with it?' she said.

'With what?'

'I'm not sure. Whatever you're talking about.'

'You know as well as I what they have to do with it.'

'I really haven't the slightest idea what you mean. Are you certain that you do yourself? Could it be that you're crazy or something?'

'It could be, but I'm not.'

'In my opinion you are.'

'You'll find out if I am or not when you come and see me.'

'I've already said that I won't come.'

'I heard what you said, but I think you will.'

'You're very sure of yourself, aren't you?'

'I'm sure that you're not such a fool as to let me talk to the police without finding out first what I have to tell them.'

'The truth is, I'm becoming rather

curious about you. It might be rather interesting to meet such an accomplished liar.'

'I'll be expecting you, then.'

'When?'

'I'm not far away. You could be here easily in fifteen minutes, but I'll give you half an hour.'

'That's very considerate of you, but I happen to have a previous engagement and can't possibly come that soon.'

'I'd advise you to break your engagement, whatever it is. I have a strong feeling that I should go to the police directly anyhow, and if you're not here within half an hour I'll go.'

'Where do you live?'

'On West Olive Street. The Cibola Apartments in the 700 block, apartment 310.'

'Well, I may come and I may not. I'll think about it.'

'Do as you please. As I said, you'll be sorry if you don't.'

'Whether I don't or do,' Willie said softly, 'it may be you who is sorry in the end.'

She hung up and wondered what to do, but all the time she knew that she was going to see Gertrude Haversack simply because she did not dare to refuse. She couldn't imagine what was on the woman's mind, but it was clearly related to Howard, whatever it was. For a breathless moment or two of terror, Willie wondered if she and Quincy could have been observed in the act of disposing of Howard by Gertrude Haversack herself, or someone else who had told her about it, but this seemed so fantastic and remote a possibility that it was surely absurd to become excessively disturbed about it. She must go and find out what this development was all about, of course, for the suspense and uncertainty would be unbearable if she didn't. But she wished desperately that there was time to talk with Quincy first; and perhaps there was, on the telephone, if she could only catch him at home or at the club without delay.

She dialed his home number, but there was no answer, and then she dialed the number of the telephone in the bar at the club. The bartender said Quincy wasn't there, but might be outside, and went to look. After a minute or two he came back and said Quincy wasn't there at all, inside or outside. There was nothing for Willie to do but go ahead to Gertrude Haversack's without talking with him.

She drove in the station wagon to West Olive Street and along the street to the 700 block. In the middle of the block, standing flush with the sidewalk and rising four stories above it, was the buff brick Cibola building. Parking at the curb about fifty feet beyond the building, Willie walked back and into a small lobby with a self-service elevator standing idle in its shaft behind closed doors, then entered the elevator and pressed the button for the third floor. She was, while rising in the shaft, surprisingly detached and oddly curious. At this time, she was more interested in seeing what kind of woman old Howard had been sleeping with, or more exactly what kind of woman had considered sleeping with old Howard a pleasure, than she was in the vastly more serious question of what Gertrude Haversack knew that she thought might concern the police.

In the third-floor hall, she looked right and left and then walked right. Apartment 310 was the third door down on the side overlooking the street. She pressed a little button set into the wall beside the door and stood listening to the buzzer inside. In order to establish a kind of imperious position, which might be a psychological advantage, she kept her finger on the button constantly until the door was opened suddenly by Gertrude Haversack, who was, Willie thought, just about the type you would picture in connection with sleeping with Howard, Willie herself excepted. She was taller than Willie and heavier, although her figure wasn't bad in an ample sort of way. She had brown hair, braided and wrapped around her head, and a rather long face which, like her figure, wasn't bad or particularly striking. It was in fact the kind of face you'd expect to see on a woman who would make a good thing out of understanding another woman's husband. Willie wasn't sure, actually, that such a woman could be expected to have a certain kind of face;

but if she could be, at any rate, the face would surely be like this one. It was the face of a woman who would try to make adultery seem like spiritual therapy.

'Are you Gertrude Haversack?' Willie said.

'That's right. I recognize you, Mrs. Hogan, even if you don't me. Please come in.'

Willie walked past her directly into a small living room, and there on a little table at the end of a sofa was a picture of Howard with his shirt open at the throat and a smile on his fat face that was plainly meant to be virile but only managed on him to look foolish. It was a shock, nevertheless, to see the picture. Willie turned her back to it, pretending that she hadn't even seen it, and faced Gertrude Haversack, who had closed the door and come back into the room a couple of steps.

'Please say whatever you have to say,' Willie said, 'for I'm in a hurry.'

'Well, you may as well sit down and be comfortable,' Gertrude Haversack said.

'No, thank you. I don't intend to stay that long.'

'I've just made some tea in the kitchen. Will you have a cup?'

Willie, who might have been seduced by a Martini, was not even tempted by tea. She shook her head and began to tap the carpet with the toe of one shoe to demonstrate her impatience. 'I don't care for any tea. I didn't come here on a social call, as you know. I've come only out of curiosity because I'm sure you must be out of your mind.'

Gertrude Haversack shrugged and sat down in a chair facing Willie and crossed her legs. She took cigarettes and paper matches out of the breast pocket of her blouse and lit one of the cigarettes with elaborate slowness, as if she thought this would irritate Willie, which it did. She blew out a cloud of smoke and waved it away with a languid motion, her hand flapping back and forth on a limp wrist.

'Suit yourself, of course. I'm prepared to be congenial, but it really makes no difference to me if you prefer it otherwise.'

'Why did you ask me to come here?'

'As I told you on the phone, I was

Howard's mistress. 'Mistress' is such an absurd word, though, to call oneself. I don't like it at all, do you? Maybe you'd rather I called myself his girl. I like that much better.'

'I don't care in the least which you call yourself, for you are probably a liar in either event.'

'Why should I lie about it? What's to be gained?'

'That's what I'm waiting to find out.'

'I was his girl. I've been his girl for almost a year, and you may as well accept it.'

'To tell the truth, I couldn't care less. It may be true, I admit, for there's no accounting for the tastes of some men.'

'You needn't be insulting. It won't help you. Do you realize how sick Howard had become of you in the last year or two?'

'I wasn't greatly concerned about it.'

'I guess you weren't. You were probably too concerned about other men. Howard said you were always getting laid by someone. He said you were no better than a whore.'

'Is that so? Well, at least I was a better

whore than the one he took up with.'

Gertrude Haversack flushed angrily and bit her lower lip, and Willie had the satisfaction of knowing that she had finally scored. She owed this bitch a jolt or two, that was certain. Perhaps she could, before this was over, think up something exceptionally unpleasant to do to her later.

'You might be interested to know that we were going away together,' Gertrude Haversack said. 'We had it all arranged. Last Friday he got together all the money he could, which amounted to about twenty thousand dollars, and Saturday evening he was coming by to pick me up. I was all ready to go, all packed and everything, and I kept waiting and waiting for him, but he didn't come. Finally I decided something had happened to change the plans, and that he would call me the first chance he got to explain what it was, but he didn't call either. The next day, Sunday, I waited again to hear from him. Then in the afternoon, a friend who knew about us called to tell me that she'd heard from someone or other that he'd left town suddenly Friday night. That's the story that's going around, that he left last Friday night and won't be back, but it's a lie. He didn't leave then because we had planned to leave together on Saturday, as I said. He had made all the arrangements, even got all that money together, and he would never have gone off without me like that at the last moment. No one knew we planned to go except him and me and this one good friend of mine, and what I want to know now is what happened to him.'

'In my opinion,' Willie said, 'you have simply made all of this up, and what you have in mind to gain from such a fantastic lie is more than I can see. Do you just want to make trouble for me?'

'I wouldn't mind making trouble for you.'

'Even if what you say is true, which I doubt, it's obvious that he merely decided to go without you. Chances are he never had any intention of taking you in the first place. As I've recently learned, Howard could be very deceptive. I'm beginning to think he probably told lots of women lies in order to get what he wanted from them.'

'You're only trying to be vindictive. He was happy with me, which he never was with you, and he wanted us to be together the rest of our lives. We were going to Mexico to live, at least until we got tired of it, and he was going to get a Mexican divorce while we were down there.'

'He may be going to Mexico, at that. I had a letter from him today from Dallas, Texas. Isn't that on the way to Mexico, more or less?'

'You had a letter from him?'

'That's what I said. From Dallas, Texas.'

'I don't believe you.'

'It's true whether you believe me or not.'

Gertrude Haversack stood up suddenly, and Willie thought for an instant that she would have to defend herself. But then the other woman became completely quiet, not moving in the slightest for several seconds, and there was an expression of slyness in her eyes. 'You could have written it yourself and had someone mail it from there. Is that what you did?'

'You really are crazy, aren't you? I see that there's no use at all in trying to talk reasonably with you.'

'I'm not crazy enough to believe for a moment that Howard would make all those careful arrangements to run away with me and then go off alone in the end. No one else will believe it, either. The police won't.'

'Won't they? I'm not so sure. You would have to prove first that he actually made such arrangements. I think you're a liar, and the police may too.'

'This friend of mine knew all about it. She'll swear it's true.'

'It isn't difficult to get a friend to lie for you. She'll only incriminate herself.'

'Think as you like. I know Howard didn't go off voluntarily without me, and I'm sure I can be convincing enough to make the police suspicious. Then they'll start asking a lot of questions they haven't asked, and start checking a lot of things they wouldn't otherwise check. Do you want that? I don't think you do. I think, in fact, that you'd do a great deal to prevent it.'

'Now we're coming to something, aren't we? You haven't told me yet just what it is you want, and it's time you did.'

'It's not so much what I want as what Howard would want. I was very fond of Howard, and I'd like to remember in the future that his wishes were considered.'

'Really? I'm touched. What were his wishes, exactly?'

'Well, it's obvious, since he was going to take care of me, that he wanted me taken care of.'

'What would you consider being taken care of?'

'He had about twenty thousand dollars. We would have shared it.'

'I see. You are trying to blackmail me for ten thousand dollars.'

'Nothing of the sort. I'm only saying that it would be no more than fair to consider Howard's wishes and take care of me as he planned.'

'Blackmail is blackmail, whatever you call it. Perhaps it's I who should go to the police.'

'Go ahead.'

'Did you really expect to get away with

this? If you did, there's one thing you forgot to take into account.'

'Is that so? What is it?'

'That I've done nothing to be black-mailed for.'

'Oh, I expected you to say that, of course. You'd hardly admit anything. If you'll think about it, though, you may decide that it's worth something to you to avoid a great deal of unpleasantness.'

Willie walked to the door and turned. She was a perfect picture of composure, and on her small gamin's face, as she stared back at Gertrude Haversack, there was an expression of fastidious disdain. She was aware of this herself, having accomplished it only by the greatest effort, and she was quite proud that she was able to dissemble so well the fear and uncertainty that she really felt. 'Have you said all you have to say?' she asked.

'For the present. I'll be waiting to hear from you.'

'Don't wait too long.'

'I won't. If I haven't heard from you by tomorrow night, I'll go to the police the next day. I want to give you every chance to do the right thing, of course.'

'Thank you so much,' Willie said. 'It's very good of you.'

She went on out and downstairs to the street. In the station wagon, she began to tremble so violently that it was impossible to drive, and so she lit a cigarette with the dash lighter, holding the lighter in her right hand and her right hand for support in her left hand. She sat there smoking the cigarette and gradually became calmer, but she was very cold in spite of the warm evening, and her hands and feet felt numb from the cold. It was essential to think clearly and to assess without panic the extent of the threat that Gertrude Haversack posed, but Willie's thoughts could not be restrained or organized and kept flying off in all directions on tangents of the most terrible possibilities. The only consistent thought she had, which did not help at all, was what a damn crying shame it was to have something like this arise just when everything was going so beautifully and looked like ending so well.

After the cigarette was finished, she

thought that she must go at once to see Quincy, who would be at the club now if he had not become tired of waiting and gone away again. Quincy was clever and full of plans. He had known what to do before, and he would know what to do now. She felt compelled to hurry, to get to him before he went away, but she drove out to the club slowly, nevertheless, for her hands still trembled a little on the wheel, and her vision, for some reason, did not seem to be very clear.

Parking in the lot in front of the club, she walked around to the back terrace, descending a flight of outside steps to the lower level. The pool was deserted, the lifeguard reading a book in his elevated seat on one side. At one end of the terrace an elderly couple were eating hamburgers, drinking beer and staring silently out across the golf course toward a little lake a hundred yards or so away. No one else was on the terrace or in sight except the guard, so Willie walked to the rear door of the club and looked through the glass into the bar; but Quincy wasn't there either. She began to tremble again in rising panic, as if her life depended upon finding Quincy at this moment and not a minute or an hour or any time later.

She opened the door and entered the bar, and then she heard a familiar sound that gave her hope. Passing through the bar and around a corner, she came to the slot-machine room; and there, sure enough, was dear little Quincy with a glass in one hand and quarters in the other. She walked across from the door and stopped beside him, and he glanced at her sidewise before depositing another quarter and pulling the handle and watching the drum whirl around.

'What's the matter, Cousin?' he said. 'You look shook.'

'I've just had a very unpleasant experience,' she said.

'Did you see old Howard's ghost or something?'

'Damn it, Quincy, please don't joke. You've got to listen to me.'

'I'm listening, Cousin. Go ahead.'

'Do you know a bitch named Gertrude Haversack?'

'No. Gertrude's a bitch I've missed. Do

you recommend her?'

'Goddamn it, Quincy, you simply must be serious.'

'Sorry, Cousin. Who's Gertrude Haversack, and besides a bitch, what?'

'Well, among other things, it seems that she was Howard's mistress.'

'Mistress? Howard's? Come off, Cousin. With apologies to present company, who the hell in her right mind would want to share a bed with old Howard?'

'I just told you. Gertrude Haversack did.'

'All right, so she did. Are you disturbed? After all, Cousin, you never seemed to put a high value on marital fidelity. What's sauce for the goose, as the saying goes, is sauce for the gander.'

'Oh, don't be ridiculous, Quincy. You're far too clever to say such foolish things just when I need your help. It makes no difference to me what Howard did, but that's not the worst of it. The worst is Howard had planned to run away with her. They were going to leave Saturday evening for Mexico. That's why he'd drawn out the money and cashed the bonds and done all those things. Now she is threatening to go to the police and tell them about it, and you can see yourself what the consequences will be. It's hardly likely that Howard would have made such elaborate plans and then simply gone off without her. It will at least make the police suspicious and troublesome.'

All this time he had been feeding quarters into the machine, pulling the handle and watching the drum spin. But now he stopped, staring at two oranges and a plum. After several seconds had passed, he took a drink from the glass in his left hand and deposited another quarter from the supply in his right. 'Correct, Cousin,' he said. 'It will at least make them suspicious and troublesome. Perhaps you had better relate your unpleasant experience with Gertrude Haversack from the beginning.'

So she did this, trying to remember every detail and word that had been said. In the meanwhile, as he listened, Quincy continued to play the machine as if she were telling the most unimportant story that was hardly worth his attention. But the whir of the spinning drum and the occasional rattle of coins served the purpose of making it impossible for her to be overheard by anyone who might come in or pass by the open door, and perhaps this was what Quincy intended, being clever and almost always anticipating contingencies.

'It's simply the rottenest kind of luck imaginable,' Willie said in finishing. 'Whoever would have expected Howard to behave that way? The bastard. Not only did he help himself to practically all our money, but he was planning to spend it on this Gertrude Haversack in Mexico. By God, Quincy, I've never encountered such deception before. All I can say is, he deserved the bitch he picked, and that's the truth. Here she was, telling me over and over how fond she was of Howard and all that, and all the while she didn't really care in the least what might have happened to him if I would only agree to give her ten thousand dollars. It was disgusting, that's what it was.'

'Oh, well,' Quincy said, 'you mustn't be indignant. You'll have to admit that we're not in a particularly good position for throwing stones. What we'd better think about is what must be done, if anything, with Gertrude Haversack.'

'That's why I came out here immediately to see you. You always have such good ideas.'

'Ideas are the products of brains, Cousin. You can't have one without the other. As I see it, we have four alternatives, which we'll consider. First, we could dispose of Gertrude as we disposed of Howard, but it hardly seems advisable. You can't go on disposing of people indefinitely without expecting to get caught, and, besides, there is this unidentified friend of Gertrude's who apparently knows what's going on. She would certainly run directly to the police if Gertrude were to disappear suddenly, and we would only have made worse what is already bad enough.

'Let's pass on, therefore, to the second alternative, which has, I confess, a quality of boldness that appeals to me. You could go to the police yourself and accuse Gertrude of trying to blackmail you. This would attract attention to you, of course, but it would give you a psychological advantage of acting like an honest woman with nothing to fear; and if Gertrude does go the police, as she threatens, attention will be attracted to you anyhow. Next, you could pay the ten thousand. Against this are the indignity of submission, the tantamount confession of guilt, and the considerable cost, which is no small item. Finally, Cousin, we could do nothing. There's always the chance that Gertrude is bluffing; and if she is, it would be unfortunate as well as humiliating to be tricked into drawing attention that could have been avoided. And in the final analysis, you have the comfort of knowing that not a damn thing can be done by the police or anyone else, whatever Gertrude says, unless someone comes up with old Howard himself, which is not probable. My advice, Cousin, is to do nothing and let Gertrude do what she will.'

Willie sighed and shook her head slowly in admiration and gratitude. She was vastly reassured by Quincy's brilliant analysis, especially the bit about Howard himself being necessary to any action by the police, which was a point she had not given sufficient attention. It was, she thought, simply incredible how this lovable and handy little devil could make everything seem all right, or almost all right, that had seemed all wrong before.

'Quincy,' she said, 'how can I ever repay you?'

'There are ways,' he said, pulling the handle of the slot machine, 'which we will go into in good time.'

14

At approximately ten o'clock Wednesday morning, Lieutenant Elgin Necessary was sitting comfortably behind his desk at police headquarters with nothing to do that had to be done immediately. He was thinking of Willie Hogan at the time, which might have been considered a coincidence, in the light of what was about to happen, if he had not been thinking of Willie practically all the time, when he was thinking at all, ever since Monday afternoon. He had even dreamed of her once, and it had been a pleasant dream, although not a dream that one would be likely to tell before breakfast, or any other time.

Thinking his pleasant thoughts — creating, in fact, a little fantasy with a beginning and an end — he was so abstracted that he was not aware he had company until Sergeant Ned Muller, who was half of it, cleared his throat to attract attention.

Necessary, returning reluctantly to reality, saw that Muller had with him a rather large young woman, well-proportioned, with an adequate face now frozen in lines of rather self-righteous determination. Necessary had seen such faces before, and his heart sank. Standing, he had a notion that he was about to acquire something to do that would need doing immediately.

Muller said: 'Lieutenant, here's a lady I think you'd better talk with. This is Lieutenant Necessary, Miss Haversack. Lieutenant, Miss Gertrude Haversack.'

Necessary extended his hand and said 'How do you do,' and Miss Haversack took the hand briefly and nodded and said nothing.

Necessary invited her to sit down in the chair beside his desk, and she said 'Thank you' and did, arranging her skirt over her knees. Sergeant Muller went away, wondering if he had performed the introduction properly. He was never quite certain afterward, and it distressed him.

'What can I do for you, Miss Haversack?' Necessary said.

'I've come to see you about a missing person,' Gertrude Haversack said.

'I see. What person is missing?'

'A friend of mine. His name is Howard Hogan. He's been missing since Friday night, I understand.'

'That's right. We've already looked into the matter, Miss Haversack. As a matter of fact, he's been located. We know, at any rate, where he was at a certain time. He sent a letter from Dallas, Texas.'

'That's what I want to talk about. I don't believe he was ever in Dallas, Texas, because I don't believe he ever left Quivera voluntarily at all.'

Necessary stared at her for a few moments sourly, his heart sinking deeper and deeper. *Oh, Jesus*, he thought. *Oh, good Jesus.* 'Why don't you believe it?' he said.

She shifted her weight in the chair, arranging her skirt over her knees again in a sort of reflexive way that was rather significant, Necessary thought, when he remembered it later in association with what she had to say.

'It's rather embarrassing,' she said. 'It

has been quite difficult for me to come here.'

'Is that why you've delayed so long in coming? As you said, Mr. Hogan left home, or disappeared, last Friday. Several days ago.'

'Yes, I suppose it is. But that's not the only reason. I kept thinking things might be satisfactorily explained in one way or another, but now I don't think so.'

'Well, now that you are here, suppose you just tell me directly why you think Mr. Hogan did not voluntarily leave town.'

'Howard — Mr. Hogan — and I were good friends. Quite good friends. We had been seeing each other regularly for about a year. To be frank, we had finally planned to go away together. We were going first to Mexico, where he planned to get a divorce. We intended to leave together last Saturday evening, and he had made all arrangements, including getting his finances in order.'

'I know. I checked that. He cleaned out his savings account and cashed some bonds.'

'I believe so. Whatever was necessary. He told me he had gotten together about twenty thousand dollars in cash.'

'That's true. About twenty thousand.'

'And now I'm expected to believe that he simply changed his mind and went off without me in the end? It makes no sense at all, and I don't believe it. Something has been done with him, and you must find out what it was.'

'Are you sure he didn't simply go away alone? Did he give any indication of becoming tired of your . . . relationship?' His pause before the final word was deliberate, prompted by an unreasonable animosity. He had the sour pleasure of seeing her flush and bite her lower lip and fuss once more with the skirt, tucking it under her knees as if she were afraid he was suddenly going to lift it.

'Not at all. There was not the slightest sign of it. Quite the contrary. On Friday, after he had been to the bank, we saw each other and made our final plans. He was eager to go.'

'How do you account for the letter from Dallas?'

'It must have been sent by someone else. Someone who was already there could have been asked to mail it, or it may even have been possible for someone to go there for that purpose.'

'The letter was received on Monday, mailed on Sunday. There was time, I suppose, for someone to get down there by air, but it seems rather unlikely.'

'Have you compared the letter with samples of Howard's handwriting?'

The question implied that he needed to be told his business, and he looked at her with his feeling of sour animosity growing stronger and stronger. The feeling was not alleviated in the least by the uneasy realization that he had, in fact, believed what he wanted to believe, and that her implied criticism was not wholly unjustified.

'There don't seem to be any samples around,' he said. 'The man apparently never wrote anything. Did he ever write to you?'

'No.'

'There it is. He had a thing about it.'

'Surely there are canceled checks,

things like that. You could at least have found samples of his signature.'

'It wouldn't have helped. The letter was typewritten.'

'Even his name at the finish?'

'That's right.'

'Doesn't that strike you as being very odd?'

Necessary admitted that it did, but he added waspishly that Mr. Hogan struck him as being rather odd in general. This made him feel slightly better; but he knew, just the same, that he had been damned negligent about a number of things in this business, not because he was lazy or stupid, but because he had not, in his heart, cared a hell of a lot about what had or had not happened to Howard Hogan, Junior.

Although he was still convinced that Howard would turn up sooner or later in his own way and time, it was obvious now that he, Necessary, would have to take steps to make it sooner if possible. He would also have to investigate further the possibility of foul play — an odious phrase — and this would be an interminable and sticky business replete with difficulties.

He sighed, although he wished mightily to curse instead, and stood up. 'You can be sure we'll continue our investigation until we are completely convinced one way or another, Miss Haversack. Thank you for coming in.'

Gertrude stood up, clutching the purse that had been lying in her lap. She may not have seen the hand that Necessary offered again in parting, but Necessary had the impression that she ignored it.

'Something has been done with Howard,' she said. 'You'll see.'

She went out, and Necessary sat down. Alone now, he did curse, as he had wished to curse before, softly and fluently.

15

Willie, advised to do nothing, was surprised to learn that doing nothing was one of the hardest things she had ever done. Not only was it hard; it was also depressing. Even painting her fingernails and toenails didn't help much. She painted them twice each day, morning and evening, a different color each time. Once she painted each nail a different color from the nail or nails beside it, using five different colors in all, but even this radical experiment in color dynamics did little to lift her depression or lessen her feeling of apprehension.

The worst part of doing nothing, she found, was that you were constantly waiting for someone else to do something. This constant waiting created a kind of tension that grew and grew inside you until you were, after a while, like a child in a dark room at night waiting for something to spring out of a corner.

All day Wednesday, which was the day Gertrude Haversack had threatened to go to the police, she kept waiting and waiting for a policeman to come or call on the telephone, possibly that queer fellow with the queer name, Lieutenant Necessary. But the day passed and no one came or called, and in the evening Gwen Festerwauld came over from next door and had a Martini.

Gwen was sober and did not have a hangover for a change, and swore to God that she was never going to drink to excess again. She asked if Willie had heard from Howard, and Willie said yes, she had; that Howard had written from Dallas, Texas. Gwen said he was probably on his way to Mexico — Tijuana, Acapulco, Mexico City, places like that — and even if Howard eventually came back, which he probably would, Willie might as well kiss that twenty grand goodbye, because the bastard would surely spend it all.

Altogether, Gwen was pretty dull, and Willie, who had been happy to see her come, was even happier to see her go. She ate dinner alone, a lamb chop and green peas and a salad that Mrs. Tweedy fixed before she left, and afterward she put the dirty dishes and silver in the kitchen sink for Mrs. Tweedy to wash when she returned in the morning. She wished that Quincy would come and keep her company, but she knew that it was Quincy's notion not to make their relationship conspicuous for a while, and so she didn't expect him to come, and he didn't.

She went into the living room and watched some television, even the fights when they came on at eight o'clock, because she thought there would be a lot of action to keep her distracted. But as it turned out, there were two bums fighting and practically no action at all.

After the fight was over, she mixed a shaker of Martinis and turned off the light, then went upstairs and undressed and put on a shortie nightgown. She was not sleepy and did not want to read, so she decided to look at pictures. She got a *Harper's Bazaar* and sat down cross-legged on the floor, opening the magazine in front of her and setting her Martini, which she had poured from the shaker, on the floor beside the magazine. She turned the pages slowly, looking carefully at the fashions and deciding that she would like to have this or wouldn't be caught dead in that, every little while taking up the glass and drinking from it and setting it down again. In about an hour, by around ten o'clock, she had gone entirely through the magazine and three Martinis.

She thought she heard a sound from Howard's bedroom beyond the bathroom, and she sat very quietly listening for the sound to repeat itself, but it didn't. Getting up from her cross-legged position without the use of her hands, which was quite a difficult thing to do, she went into the bathroom, where she stood for a few minutes bent forward in an attitude of listening. But there was still no sound, of course, for there had been none to start with except in her imagination.

Standing there, she had again the feeling that she had only to open the door suddenly to cancel out in an instant everything that had happened since last Friday night and to restore Howard to life, yawning and scratching on his way to bed. She didn't open the door, however, for it would be a significant concession, a very bad sign, to yield to such fantasies by testing them. Instead, she went back into her bedroom and poured what was left in the Martini shaker into her glass and sat down on the edge of the bed. She began to think of Quincy, and what a remarkably effective little devil he was in solving problems and making love. Presently she was thinking of him in the latter capacity exclusively, and she wished very much that he was here.

As late as it was, it would surely do no harm for him to come, if he was careful, and it would be a comfort and pleasure to her that he surely wouldn't deny if she were to ask it. Having finished the last Martini, she went out into the hall and dialed his number. 'Quincy,' she said when he answered, 'what are you doing?'

'I'm sitting here in my pajamas and reading De Quincy's *Confessions of an English Opium Eater*.'

'What's that?'

'It's a piece by a man who ate opium.'

'Why are you reading it?'

'Originally I read it to find out what an opium eater had to confess, but now I'm reading it again because it amuses me.'

'It doesn't sound very amusing, if you ask me.'

'I didn't ask you, Cousin, but I'm glad to have your opinion.'

'It would be much more amusing if you came over to keep me company.'

'Is that guaranteed?'

'Yes, it is.'

'It's tempting, I admit, but not very discreet.'

'Please come, Quincy. I'm lonesome and depressed and would be grateful if you would.'

'All right, Cousin. I'll be there pretty soon.'

'I'll leave the front door unlocked for you.'

She went downstairs from the telephone and unlocked the front door, and while she was there she thought she might as well mix some more Martinis, but she had left the shaker upstairs. Never mind, however. She could mix them as well in a pitcher. She went into the kitchen and got one and some ice, and carried them into the living room where she'd left the open bottles. After mixing a generous batch of Martinis, she turned out all the down-stairs lights, except a dim one at the foot of the stairs in the hall, and went up to her room again, where she sat the pitcher on the floor beside her empty glass. She sat down before the glass and the pitcher, as she had sat before the magazine a while ago, and she thought that she would wait for Quincy before having another Martini to drink. But after waiting and waiting for an interminable time, she decided that she had better go ahead and have another to help pass the time until he arrived.

She leaned forward without uncrossing her legs to pour it, and she had drunk it all, even though she drank it slowly in sips to make it last, before she heard the door open into the hall below and Quincy's footsteps ascending the stairs.

'Quincy,' she said when he entered the room, 'I thought you were never coming. What on earth kept you?'

'Nothing kept me. It takes a while to

walk out here from my place, you know.'

'Did you walk? Why?'

'Well, since it's already late and will probably be a lot later before I leave, I thought it would be just as well not to have my car parked in the drive for someone to see.'

'Oh. I should have thought of that myself. You're very clever to always think of these things, Quincy.'

'We had better think of things, Cousin, if we want to stay out of trouble. Why the hell are you sitting on the floor?'

'I like to sit on the floor. It relaxes me. Will you sit beside me and have a Martini?'

'I'll have a Martini, but I prefer to sit on the bed, if you don't mind.'

'All right. I'll sit on the bed with you. There's another glass on my dressing table there.'

Bending forward, she picked up the pitcher and rose without the use of hands from the floor. At the dressing table after the glass, he watched her in the mirror with admiration that was inspired partly by the trick of getting up that way, but mostly by her appearance in the shortie nightgown.

He held his glass and hers while she poured, and then they sat down beside each other on the edge of the bed. She leaned against him and sighed and let her head fall sidewise onto his shoulder, and he put his right arm around her waist.

'Quincy?' she said.

'Yes, Cousin?'

'Everything will be all right, won't it?'

'I think so.'

'Will Gertrude Haversack cause me trouble?'

'She may try.'

'Do you think she will succeed?'

'I don't think so.'

'Today was the day she said she'd go to the police.'

'Have you heard from them?'

'No.'

'You see? She may not have gone at all.'

'I was feeling depressed before you came, but now I'm not.'

'It must be the Martini.'

'No. It's you.'

'Thanks, Cousin.'

'I can't begin to tell you what a comfort you are to me.'

'I suppose it's better to be a comfort than nothing.'

'A comfort's not all. You are a comfort besides.'

'Besides what?'

'Besides an excitement.'

'That's much better. Are you excited now?'

'I'm beginning to be.'

★   ★   ★

She did not know, later, when he left. She had sunk softly on a sense of spurious security into the most delicious sleep, and when she wakened in the early morning hours, long before daylight, he was gone.

The vast expanse of bed beside her was terrifyingly empty, and she was lonelier in that instant than she had ever been before. In her loneliness, after a while, she went back to sleep.

16

After lunch that day, Thursday, Gwen Festerwauld called and said it was such a nice day she was wondering if Willie would like to play nine holes of golf, or maybe eighteen if they felt like going ahead with it, and Willie said she would. It wasn't exactly true that she really wanted to play golf with Gwen, but it was something better to do than nothing, and Gwen was someone better to do it with than no one, and so they went out in Gwen's car about two o'clock.

Willie was a bad golfer, but Gwen was worse, and usually when they played together they didn't even bother to keep score unless they had an agreement that the loser would pay for the drinks or something after they were finished. Today Willie was bored with the game after two holes and with Gwen after three, but it was pleasant out on the course with its clipped green grass and big splashes of shade under trees here and there to rest in. It was much hotter in the sun than they had anticipated, however, and so they decided to quit after nine holes and go into the club bar for the drinks that Gwen had to pay for, being the loser; or rather to sign for, Marv actually being the loser when you came to think of it.

As it turned out, neither Gwen nor Marv had to pay for the drinks, because Evan Spooner was in the bar and picked up the tab. Evan hadn't had much to do with Willie since the day Howard had kicked his butt right out of the house, but it was pretty apparent now, since Howard was reported to have run away and left an open field, that he was prepared to give Willie her fair share of his attention again.

But Willie wasn't interested. Although she was polite and permitted him to buy her drinks, it was impossible to look at Evan now without seeing him being kicked by Howard. You'd have thought that Evan himself would be too ashamed to come near her, let alone expect serious consideration, but he was nearly impervious to shame and wasn't even embarrassed. Anyhow, all this aside, Willie wasn't interested because she had been spoiled by Quincy.

It was cool and pleasant in the bar, and Willie and Gwen sat in there with Evan for quite a long time. But after a while the situation became somewhat strained, because Evan kept talking with Willie and practically ignored Gwen, and Gwen kept getting more and more annoyed and finally began making remarks about being bored and wanting to go home. After so much of this, Evan asked her why the hell she didn't go, and quit talking about it. Gwen said she was damn well going and told Willie to come on, and Evan said he would be glad to take Willie home later if she wanted to stay, but Willie didn't.

She went out with Gwen and started back home in Gwen's car. 'That Evan Spooner is a goddamn bore,' Gwen said.

'Yes, he is,' Willie said. 'He really is.'

'Marv hates his guts.'

'So did Howard.'

'Where does he get off, being so conceited? The bastard thinks if he died all the girls would wear their pants at half-mast.'

Willie thought this was funny, and began to laugh. Having started laughing, she had trouble stopping, and Gwen was so pleased by the success of her remark that she began at once to regain her good humor. By the time she pulled into her drive across the hedge from Willie's, she was her usual congenial self.

'Hadn't you ever heard that before?' she said. 'About the girls wearing their pants at half-mast?'

'No, I hadn't heard it.'

'Oh, it's an old one. I didn't make it up.'

'It certainly fits Evan, anyhow. That's just what he'd think.'

'He's unsure of himself, that's his trouble. Men who are unsure of themselves are forever trying to lay every woman they meet in an effort to prove their competence. I happen to know someone who got tight and let him lay her, and this person says he's absolutely no good at all.'

Willie could have contributed something on this point, but she did, of course, nothing of the sort. 'Well,' she said, 'I think I'd better get on home. Thanks for the game.'

'Won't you come in and have another drink?'

'I don't think I'd better. I'll see you later, Gwen.'

She got her clubs out of the back of Gwen's car and went around the hedge and into the house. It was, she noticed, even later than she'd thought. It was, in fact, about five thirty, and she had forgotten to give Mrs. Tweedy any instructions about dinner — whether there should be any and what time, if any, it should be — and Mrs. Tweedy, whose sympathy could be imposed on only so far, had gone away early in a huff instead of waiting to find out. She had, however, left a note propped against the telephone in the hall, and the note, after stating Mrs. Tweedy's rather bitter assumption that Willie must not have planned to eat in, since she hadn't bothered to say, said further that there had been a telephone call from a Lieutenant Elgin Necessary at police headquarters, and Lieutenant Necessary would appreciate it if Willie would call him back just as soon as she got in, and it gave the number to dial.

It was perfectly apparent what had happened. Gertrude Haversack, the bitch, had gone to the police after all, in spite of Quincy's feeling that she might not, and now it would be necessary to answer more questions and explain things that Willie had hoped would not need explaining.

What she could not quite understand was why Necessary had waited so long to contact her after talking with Gertrude Haversack. But perhaps he hadn't; perhaps Gertrude had not gone to him as soon as she'd threatened — perhaps only today. And anyhow, now that she had obviously gone, the essential thing was to keep calm and decide deliberately what attitude to take regarding what Gertrude had surely told.

On the whole, Willie thought, it would be best to take the attitude that Gertrude was probably a liar, although possibly not; and that she, Willie, in the latter event, could hardly be expected to grieve because Howard had deceived his mistress, as well as his wife, in a miserable little affair that was a complete surprise to almost everyone.

Having decided this, she dialed the number and got a Sergeant Muller, who put Necessary on. 'Good evening, Mrs. Hogan,' he said. 'I've been waiting for your call.'

'I've just gotten home. I was out at the country club playing golf this afternoon.'

'So I was told, but I thought there was no need to interrupt your game.'

'That's very considerate of you, I'm sure. Is there something I can do for you?'

'I wonder if you'll do me the favor of coming down here for a little talk.'

'This evening?'

'I'd appreciate it very much.'

'Isn't it rather late?'

'It is, rather, but something important has come up that we should discuss as soon as possible.'

'What has come up?'

'I'd prefer not to discuss it on the telephone, if you'll excuse me. If you wish, I'll have you picked up in a police car.'

Necessary spoke softly and courteously,

signifying by inflection his regret of being compelled by duty to intrude; but Willie did not misunderstand, nevertheless, the true meaning of his offer to have her picked up and delivered. He meant that he would do so if she declined to come voluntarily by her own means. He had in kindness permitted her to finish her golf game, but that, apparently, was the limit of his concession.

'That won't be necessary,' Willie said. 'I'll drive myself down.'

'I hope you'll be able to come right away,' he said.

Meaning, she thought, that she'd damn well better. She said she would, and hung up. After hanging up, she immediately lifted the phone again and dialed Quincy's number to tell him where she was going and to ask his advice; but Quincy wasn't home, or didn't answer if he was, and she decided not to try the numbers of any of the other places he might be. She was not, anyhow, especially apprehensive. Nothing had happened except what she had been expecting to happen, and it was actually a relief that it finally had.

As Quincy had said with his remarkable facility for going directly to the heart of a matter, nothing could be proven or done without Howard, and Howard was not available.

Besides, Necessary had not seemed at all threatening. On the contrary, he had been, although determined, courteous and kind and apparently friendly.

17

She drove downtown in the station wagon and parked in a small paved lot beside City Hall, in which the police headquarters were located. Inside, Sergeant Muller, who was waiting for her, escorted her to the desk of Lieutenant Necessary, who was also waiting for her. While Muller was retreating, relieved this time of the obligation to perform an introduction, Necessary unfolded upward from his chair and held out a hand. He resisted a desire to hold Willie's overlong, and to hold it, for the brief time that he did, more tightly than was proper.

'Thanks for coming so promptly, Mrs. Hogan,' he said. 'Please sit down.'

'I'm glad to cooperate in any way I can,' Willie said, 'but I hope you won't keep me too long.'

'I'll be as brief as I can.'

Willie sat down in the chair beside the desk and crossed her legs, and Necessary was almost positive that the knee on top was dimpled. Dimpled knees, he thought, were rather rare and peculiarly seductive. He wished he could verify the dimple at his leisure, but he could allow himself only the first quick and insufficient look.

'I have some information,' he said, looking at his hands, which he laid on his desk, 'that I feel I should discuss with you.'

'I know what it is,' she said.

'You know?'

'I think so. It's about Gertrude Haversack.'

'Have you known about Gertrude Haversack long?'

'No, only since Monday. She called me and asked me to come and see her, and I went.'

'What did she want to see you about?'

'She said that she and Howard had planned to leave town together last Saturday. She said she didn't believe Howard would leave without her, after making plans and everything for them to leave together. She seemed to have some ridiculous notion that something had happened to Howard and that I was somehow responsible.'

'I see. Well, granting the truth of what she claims about your husband and her making such plans, it does seem odd, to say the least, that he would suddenly abandon them.'

'Do you think so? It all depends upon your point of view, I suppose.'

'What do you mean?'

'Frankly, after meeting Gertrude Haversack I don't find it at all odd that a man should decide not to run away with her. I only find it odd that he should have considered it in the first place.'

This was so precisely Necessary's secret attitude that he felt for a moment a sense of communication with Willie that alleviated briefly the sour sickness of heart that was his basic feeling. 'Nevertheless,' he said, 'it seems certain that your husband maintained a relationship with Miss Haversack for some time, and it is not unlikely that they did have plans to leave town together.'

'Perhaps it's true. If you say so, I'm willing to concede it.'

'You don't seem particularly concerned.'

'Should I be? He was deceptive and dishonest with me, taking all that money which was rightly half mine, and now it turns out that he was just as deceptive with Gertrude Haversack.'

'You think, then, that he deliberately lied to her?'

'That seems apparent, doesn't it? Probably he only made a lot of promises to get what he wanted from her before he left.'

'She's convinced that he didn't.'

'Are you sure? Naturally she'd say that. It's humiliating to a woman to be discarded.'

'I must say, Mrs. Hogan, that *you* don't impress me as being humiliated.'

'That's because I wasn't discarded. Not really. It was different with Howard and me.'

'How different?'

'I'd prefer not to go into it. It wouldn't help you to know.'

'Are you suggesting that you had, in effect, already discarded *him*, and that his action was only a kind of final acceptance of it?'

'You may put it that way if you like.'

'All right. Can you tell me why Miss Haversack discussed this business with you in the first place? Did she expect you to explain why your husband failed to carry out their plans?'

'No. She had the ridiculous notion that something had happened to him that I was responsible for.'

'In that case, why didn't she come first to the police?'

'Because she wanted to try to blackmail me for ten thousand dollars to get her to keep quiet.'

Necessary had been looking alternately at her and at his hands, and now he looked up from his hands with a sharp jerk of his head and looked at her steadily for several seconds before speaking. 'Do you understand what you're saying?' he said.

'Of course I understand. I'm quite capable of understanding myself, thank you.'

'Then why didn't *you* come to the police? Blackmail's a crime.'

'Because it was so perfectly silly. I'd

done nothing wrong, and I simply decided to ignore it. I didn't want a lot of unpleasantness. The truth is, I thought she was one of these crazy people you read about. After I left her, I didn't expect to hear from her again.'

'Well, she must have had some reason for trying such a thing. She must have had some reason for *thinking* you would be vulnerable.'

'You'd think so, wouldn't you? That's why I decided she must be crazy. Crazy people don't have reasons for thinking something. Only crazy reasons, anyhow.'

He spread the fingers of his hand on his desk, staring at them morosely, and his sour sickness of heart, he thought, was seeping from his pores into the close air of the room, so that he could smell himself, his sour sickness, and he did not like the smell. Suddenly he looked up again with that peculiar jerk of his head. 'Mrs. Hogan,' he said, 'do you know a young woman by the name of Stemple? Fidelity Stemple?'

She knew at once that she knew no one of that name well, but she thought carefully before answering in an effort to remember if it might be someone she had known slightly at one time, if not now. However, she could remember no one at all with either the first name or last name he mentioned. It was an unusual name, Fidelity, and she was certain that she would remember anyone she had ever known who was called that.

'No,' she said, 'but I didn't know Gertrude Haversack, either, before Monday. I hope it's not someone else Howard has been involved with.'

'It's not. This young woman is dead. She was killed last night in an automobile accident a couple of hundred miles from here.'

'That's very sad, I'm sure; but what has it to do with me? Why did you ask me if I knew her?'

He stared at her and shook his head as if he was bewildered and did not know himself why he had asked. 'I don't know. I thought you might. Do you know a man named Fred Honeyburg?'

This time there were echoes in her brain, elusive and disturbing. She was almost positive that she had heard the name before, but she could not remember where or when or in what connection, and it was in that instant, hearing the echoes, that she had the most terrible conviction that everything that had been going right had suddenly started going wrong and would get as bad as it could be. In unconscious resistance to the conviction, she straightened in her chair in a posture of prim rigidity, folding her hands in her lap. 'I can't remember anyone of that name,' she said, 'and I wish you would tell me why you are asking me these strange questions about strange people.'

'Possibly they're strange questions about strange people because they're related to a strange story,' he said. 'As I told you, Fidelity Stemple was killed in an automobile accident last night. Fred Honeyburg was driving the car she was riding in. Honeyburg wasn't hurt much. Bruises and abrasions, as the expression is. Funny thing is, the car he was driving was your husband's. A check of the license proved that. And to make the story stranger still, he claims he was asked to steal the car early last Sunday morning from the KC Municipal Parking Lot, and the person who asked him to steal it was his own cousin, who was also the cousin of your husband on the other side of the family, whose name is Quincy Hogan of Quivera. Do you know Quincy Hogan, Mrs. Hogan?'

She sat there rigidly with her hands folded, and she was thinking with a kind of bitter clarity, as if a tiny thinking part of her brain were somehow detached from the stricken remainder that even the cleverest plans must certainly go wrong if you are deceived on every side by those you had thought reliable. She had been deceived by Howard, who had behaved in a way she hadn't anticipated; and Quincy, clever as he was, had been deceived by his cousin on his mother's side, who had failed to keep his agreement regarding the Buick. Such deception could not be predicted or dealt with. She sat alone in ruins, but to Necessary, watching her, she seemed so calm and demurely immune that his heart lifted in the hope that she was innocent, after all, of what he had begun to think her guilty.

'Yes,' she said. 'Of course I know him. How could I help it when he lives right here in town?'

'Do you know how he got hold of your husband's car?'

'No. I can't imagine.'

'Or why he left it in a certain place by arrangement to be stolen?'

'No. What can it possibly mean?'

'That's what I'm wondering.'

'I'm sorry. I can't tell you.'

'No idea at all?'

'It seems so senseless, doesn't it? Do you think Howard and Quincy could have met after Howard left home last Friday night?'

'Possibly. Are you suggesting that Quincy may have done away with your husband and then disposed of the car in this way? It sounds pretty devious.'

'Well, Quincy's clever, but he's very odd. No one ever knows quite what he's thinking or what he will do next.'

'What reason could he have had for harming your husband?'

'None that I know of. Could it have

been for the money Howard had?'

'The twenty thousand, you mean? That's a lot of money, all right. How would you explain the letter from Dallas?'

'Perhaps it was a trick to get everyone to quit wondering about Howard. Do you think it could have been?'

'I think it could. I think it was. However, I'm positive that Quincy did not meet your husband and kill him after he left your home on Friday night.'

'Are you? Why?'

'There's the car, for one thing. It wasn't left in the lot in KC until early Sunday morning. Where was it in the meanwhile?'

'I have no idea.'

'Don't you, Mrs. Hogan? I do. I have an idea it was in the garage at your home on Ouichita Road.'

She sat quietly again, her hands folded and her head bowed, and she looked so small and forlorn that he wanted to lean forward and touch her and tell her that he was only guessing, after all, and that probably none of what he said was true, or at least he hoped it wasn't.

She sat unmoving for quite a long while in a silence that became oppressive, and she seemed to be thinking or praying or searching for something within herself. But what she was actually doing, in the ruins of her hope, was making a last desperate canvass of possible positions, the evasion or the truth or the lie that would help her most when help in fact seemed gone. After a while, she looked up with a sigh and a sad little smile that trembled on her lips.

'I see I must tell you the truth,' she said.

'I think you must,' he said.

'I had hoped to save him, but now I see that I can't.'

'Save who, Mrs. Hogan?'

'Cousin Quincy.'

'What about Cousin Quincy?'

'In order to make you understand, I'll have to tell you some personal matters that I had rather not have to tell.'

'I'm sorry. I'll treat whatever you tell me as confidentially as possible.'

'Well, to begin with, Howard had this idea that Quincy and I were in love with each other, or were having a kind of affair at least; and the truth is, I *am* very fond of Quincy, who is clever and charming when you get to know him. There was nothing in it, though, that should have upset Howard and made him so absolutely unreasonable. He was simply furious and kept accusing me of things. And then there was this party at the club last Friday night.

'Howard and Quincy were there. About midnight I went outside for some fresh air and met Quincy, who had gone out ahead of me. We talked and took a little walk, then came back to the club, and Howard had gone home without me. There was nothing for Quincy to do but take me home in his car, which he did. When we got there, he decided that he had better come in and try to explain to Howard and see to it, anyhow, that Howard didn't abuse me or beat me, which he had done before. It was a mistake for him to go in, as it turned out, for Howard was in a perfect rage, practically out of his mind, and he had this little gun he was going to shoot me with. When Quincy came in, however, he was determined to shoot Quincy first, but Quincy leaped on him suddenly and took the gun away. Perhaps you wouldn't think Quincy would be capable, as he's so small, but he was actually incredibly fierce and quick.

'Howard, for his part, was a lunatic. He shouted and charged at Quincy and grabbed him by the throat with the intention of strangling him, and so Quincy shot him, naturally, in order to save himself. Afterward he took Howard away and disposed of him. I tried to convince him that he should call the police and tell exactly what had happened, that it was self-defense and all. But he said no, that no one would believe it. So because he had been so brave and had saved my life from Howard, who would have killed me, I agreed to keep quiet; and I have, up till now. That's the way it was and how it happened.'

From Necessary's heart, the lift, the last sad hope, was gone. He wagged his head slowly from side to side, a gesture of definitive concession. 'And so,' he said, 'you became an accessory to save him.'

'I know it was wrong, and I'm sorry, but I had to do it.'

'Yet only a few minutes ago you were suggesting that he met your husband that night and killed him for the twenty thousand dollars that he presumably had on his person. If you will excuse my saying so, Mrs. Hogan, you seem to be confused.'

She knew, of course, that she had done very badly, in spite of trying so very hard to do well. Now there was nothing more to say that would undo what had foolishly been said and done. But she said, nevertheless, with the peculiar and culminating courage of desperation, the only thing that she could think to say. 'I was frightened,' she said. 'I hope you will understand and pay no attention to it.'

'I'm afraid I don't,' he said. 'I'm afraid I don't understand at all. Do you, Mr. Hogan?'

He was looking up and beyond her now, over her shoulder, and she turned and looked in the same direction, but there was no one there. There was only a closed door that opened into the next room. She turned back to find Necessary staring at the door as if he were expecting someone to open it at any moment. Someone did open it, in fact, and stood behind her without speaking; and it was then, at the moment of the door's opening, that she became fully aware for the first time of the little box on Necessary's desk: an intercom.

Everything they had said, she understood, had been overheard in the next room by Quincy himself and probably another policeman, and it was Quincy to whom Necessary had spoken, and Quincy now standing behind her. She stood up and turned and looked at him with a little smile, lifting her hands in a gesture of entreaty, and she thought that he was somehow smaller than she had remembered, thin and frail.

'Quincy,' she said, 'Lieutenant Necessary doesn't believe me. Please tell him that I told the truth.'

He shook his head, smiling, and the smile seemed to be an acceptance of the damned and perverse nature of things in general. 'Sorry, Cousin. Old Fred has put me in an untenable position, goddamn him.

I'm afraid I must begin to protect myself.'

'Are you trying to put the blame on me, Quincy, after all I've done to save you?'

He continued to shake his head, still smiling. 'It won't work, Cousin. I have the gun, you see. I kept it as insurance, with your fingerprints nicely preserved, for just such a contingency as this. I must say, however, that I hoped never to use it.'

Necessary stood up. His movements gave the effect of carefully controlled violence. Looking at Quincy, he kept seeing Willie. His feeling for her was not merely ambivalent. It was so complex, composed of such diverse and conflicting elements, that it made him feel grotesque, physically and mentally monstrous.

'Where is the gun?' he said, 'and where is Howard Hogan?'

'You will find the gun in my apartment,' Quincy said. 'As for old Howard, you'll have to dig for him.'

18

Willie sat in the visitors' room of the Quivera County jail. She had been there for some time, talking with Mr. Greenbaum, who was now making some notes in a notebook with a black leather cover. Released from the necessity to listen and respond, Willie looked up and out through a high window into the green leaves of an oak tree. She could see a couple of sparrows among the leaves, and she could hear the comfortable scratching of Mr. Greenbaum's pen.

It was absolutely remarkable, Willie thought, how kind everyone had been. At first she had been frightened and depressed all the time, but now she was frightened and depressed only part of the time, and the rest of the time she had the most wonderfully serene feeling that everything would come out all right in the end, after all.

Take Mr. Greenbaum, for instance. He

was really a big lawyer from KC. She had not expected to have such a lawyer, but then someone had started a collection in Quivera to hire him for Willie, and it was the truth that thousands of dollars had been collected from all sorts of people in practically no time. Then a committee had gone to KC to ask Mr. Greenbaum to take the case, and Mr. Greenbaum had made an eloquent little speech of acceptance, saying how he could do no less than reflect the faith of these good citizens in Willie's innocence. It had been in the KC papers and other papers all over the country.

The daily paper of Quivera had been more than fair and kind. Of course, a newspaper couldn't come right out and express a conviction one way or the other in a matter like this, because it wouldn't be fair to the other side; but it was made pretty plain, just the same, whose side exactly the Quivera paper was on. Quite a lot was written and published about Howard's unreasonable jealousy and abuse, and particularly about how he'd tried to get away with the money, which was practically stealing, and morally wrong, if not legally.

Officials at the jail had been very nice about bringing in the papers and letting Willie read the stories, which were encouraging and exciting. The pictures of herself were very satisfying, because she was naturally photogenic. But ever more encouraging and exciting and satisfying had been what had happened when she was taken at different times from the jail to the county court house for questioning by the county attorney. Each time, the news had leaked out somehow, and there were crowds of people all along the way, going and coming, shouting their support and blowing kisses. Altogether, it had made her feel exhilarated and humble and almost like crying.

What had made her feel most like crying, however, was the episode involving Tommy Cochran, which was a kind of demonstration, it seemed to her, of the way almost everyone seemed to feel. Tommy Cochran was a reporter for the Quivera paper, a young Irishman with black curly hair and blue eyes; and one night in her cell, which was on the second-floor rear of the jail, she had looked out through the bars to see what had happened to the moonlight that had suddenly stopped coming in, and there was Tommy in the way of the light. At first she was terrified, and couldn't imagine how he'd got there. But luckily she hadn't screamed, and it turned out that he'd climbed up a big elm in the yard and out along a limb, from which he'd jumped over onto the flat roof. He had a coil of rope, and he tied one end around a chimney and dropped the other over the side. Then he slid down the rope to her window, and that was how he'd got there.

What he had in mind was to get her out and run away with her. He said he had it all thought through. They would go, he said, to New Orleans, where they would catch a boat to a certain country in South America that had no extradition treaty with the United States. He asked her if she would agree to go, and she said yes, of course, because he had gone to so much trouble, and because it was a night when she was feeling frightened and depressed.

He said he would be back the next night with a hacksaw to begin sawing the bars. And sure enough, he was back and began sawing, wrapping a heavy cloth around the saw to muffle the sound. It might actually have come off successfully, which would have been tremendously exciting, if he had not unfortunately fallen to the ground and broken his back, besides several other bones. He didn't die, she was told later, but it was likely he would be paralyzed for the rest of his life from the waist down.

Well, Tommy Cochran was just an example of the way people seemed to feel about her. Even Gwen Festerwauld had come to see her and tell her how she remembered Howard's shouting threats and accusations at various times. Gwen hadn't actually realized that they were threats and accusations when she'd heard Howard shout them, but now she did, looking back, and she was prepared to swear to it if necessary; and Marv would damn well swear to it, if he knew what was good for him.

It was no wonder that Willie felt, on the whole, serene and hopeful most of the time, as she felt now, watching the sparrows in the leaves and listening to the scratching of Mr. Greenbaum's pen. The pen, however, had stopped scratching, and she lowered her eyes to see the great lawyer watching her with a fatherly expression.

'I must be going now,' Mr. Greenbaum said, 'but let us be certain first that we understand our basic position. Your husband was unreasonably jealous and frequently violent. He threatened several times to kill you, and you had become afraid of him, although you suffered your fear in silence in the hope of saving your marriage. The night of his death, after he deliberately deserted you for no good reason, you came home to find him waiting in a deadly rage. He accused you falsely of infidelity and said he intended to kill you. That this intent was, in fact, premeditated, and had been so for some time, is supported by the preparations for flight that he had obviously made. He came toward you with his hands outstretched. He was, in your judgment, beyond reason. In your terror, you remembered the gun in the bedside table. You ran there, took the gun, fired. Your husband dropped dead with a bullet in his heart. Afterward, not knowing what to do, you called your Cousin Quincy, who was your good friend. Upon his advice — which was ill-taken, perhaps — you decided to dispose of the body with his help, becoming involved in some rather incredible ramifications; and this foolish act was, in reality, your only crime. This is the whole truth, isn't it, my dear?'

She nodded, looking up again at the sparrows among the leaves. 'It sounds like a bad dream doesn't it? Do you think the jury will believe it?'

Leaning forward, he took one of her hands in one of his. In his big palm, the little hand was almost lost. He squeezed it gently.

'I think so, Willie,' he said. 'I really think they will.'

We do hope that you have enjoyed reading this large print book.

Did you know that all of our titles are available for purchase?

We publish a wide range of high quality large print books including:
Romances, Mysteries, Classics
General Fiction
Non Fiction and Westerns

Special interest titles available in large print are:
The Little Oxford Dictionary
Music Book, Song Book
Hymn Book, Service Book

Also available from us courtesy of Oxford University Press:
Young Readers' Dictionary
(large print edition)
Young Readers' Thesaurus
(large print edition)

For further information or a free brochure, please contact us at:
Ulverscroft Large Print Books Ltd.,
The Green, Bradgate Road, Anstey,
Leicester, LE7 7FU, England.
Tel: (00 44) **0116 236 4325**
Fax: (00 44) **0116 234 0205**

GIRL MEETS BOY

Jack Iams

Reunited with his English war bride, Sybil, after two years, Tim takes her back to the USA with him — but where to live, in the middle of the post-World War II housing crisis? They meet a friend of Sybil's deceased father, who promises to help. Next thing they know, the New Jersey chapter of the British-American War Brides Improvement Association arranges accommodation for them in the isolated coastal community of Merry Point. Here they meet their curmudgeonly landlord and an inept handyman. Then Sybil finds a body on the pier . . .